MONSTER HUNT

ERIC S BROWN

SEVERED PRESS
HOBART TASMANIA

MONSTER HUNT

CHARACTER PROFILES

WALT

Strength: 35
Accuracy: 38
Speed: 30
Intelligence: 43
Endurance/Damage Points: 44
Class: Leader
Notes: Exceptional skill rating in use of AK-47 assault rifle.

SARAH

Strength: 25
Accuracy: 46
Speed: 50
Intelligence: 35
Endurance/Damage Points: 39
Class: Gunslinger
Notes: Exceptional skill rating in all handguns (pistols/revolvers).
Exceptional skill rating in speed loading. Exceptional skill rating
in knife throwing. Gifted skill rating in swordsmanship (Plus 5
point bonus when applied to katana use).

LEE

Strength: 35
Accuracy: 35
Speed: 40
Intelligence: 30
Endurance/Damage Points: 27
Class: Adventurer
Notes: Exceptional skill rating in lock picking. Exceptional skill
rating in demolitions. Exceptional skill rating in first aid.

BRENT

Strength: 50
Accuracy: 38
Speed: 25
Intelligence: 20
Endurance/Damage Points: 49
Class: Brute
Notes: Exceptional skill rating in weight lifting. Exceptional skill rating hand-to-hand combat.

CALLY

Strength: 19
Accuracy: 30
Speed: 35
Intelligence: 50
Endurance/Damage Points: 24
Class: Tech
Notes: Exceptional skill rating in science. Exceptional skill rating in technology. Exceptional skill rating in jury-rigging. Gifted skill rating in computers.

SIMON

Strength: 40
Accuracy: 50
Speed: 44
Intelligence: 35
Endurance/Damage Points: 40
Class: Sniper
Notes: Gifted skill rating in all firearms. Exceptional skill rating in stealth.

THE BEAST

Strength: 100
Max. Speed: 80 MPH
Endurance/Damage Points: 150
The Beast is a modified, six wheeled, armored personnel carrier.
Capable of all terrain travel. Hidden topside missile launcher.
Concealed, forward-facing anti-personnel machine guns.
Concealed flamethrower unit in center of forward grill. The Beast
serves as means of transport not only on each level of the game but
as the instantaneous means of transport for the team to the game's
central Hub area when activated at the end of each level.

ENTERING GAME IN PROGRESS ...

The crossbow twanged as Sarah took her shot. The bolt flew straight and true, penetrating the dead man's skull. His body flopped against the wall of the corridor before tumbling to rest on the floor.

"Sarah! Look out!" Brent screamed as another of the zombies emerged behind her from one of the side rooms that ran the length of the corridor.

Sarah spun about and saw the woman. She had to have been killed recently. The blood slicking the front of her dress from her torn-out throat was still wet. The woman's glazed-over eyes were locked onto her, her teeth already snapping together in anticipation of the taste of Sarah's flesh. Sarah spun to meet the woman. There was no time to reload her crossbow so she used it as a club trying to keep the dead woman away from her. The butt of the crossbow smacked into the side of the dead woman's head, causing her to stumble. The dead woman recovered more quickly from the blow than Sarah had expected, cold hands reaching towards her.

Brent stepped between the dead woman and Sarah, the barrel of his Glock flashing in the dim light of the corridor as he squeezed the pistol's trigger. The backside of the dead woman's skull exploded as the high-caliber round exited it. A shower of gore splattered in the air.

"These effects are freaking awesome!" Lee yelled from the far end of the corridor where he hosed a group of the dead with his P-90, emptying the weapon's fifty-round magazine into them. Their bodies twitched and lurched about as the bullets tore into them.

"Headshots, you idiot!" Walt shouted. "They're the only way to kill these things. Don't you know anything about zombies?"

Lee was laughing as he popped the spent magazine from his P-90 and slammed a fresh one into the weapon. "Get a grip, Walt! Some of us like to have a little fun!"

"Watch it, Lee!" Walt snapped. "You're going to get us all killed!"

Lee looked up to see most of the zombies he had shot still lumbering towards him. His eyes bugged at how close they were. His first barrage of fire had dropped a few and slowed the pack of dead folks down but that was it. They had crept closer to him as he reloaded without him noticing.

"Frag me!" Lee shouted and took off running away from the pack of dead creatures.

Walt was blocking his path. "Where do you think you're going? We have to get out of here alive and blow this place if we want to beat this level."

"Clear this way!" Brent's voice boomed from behind where Walt and Lee stood.

"Roger that!" Walt called out as he yanked a grenade from his belt, pulling its pin. He lobbed into the mass of dead creatures coming at him and Lee. "Get down!"

Walt shoved Lee to the corridor's floor as the grenade detonated in a flash of fire and shrapnel that sent bits of zombies spinning away from the center of the blast. The explosion ripped a hole in the frontlines of the dead creatures' ranks. As the sound of it echoed in the corridor, Walt was already pulling Lee to his feet with one hand and firing his AK-47 on full auto into the creatures that had survived the explosion from the grenade. He hated wasting ammo in such a fashion, but if he didn't keep pouring fire into the things to hold them back, he knew that he and Lee would be overrun before they could get moving.

Lee shook Walt's hand off of him and brought up his P-90 level at the remainder of the approaching creatures. The weapon chattered and blazed as he and Walt made a fighting retreat towards where Brent and Sarah were waiting on them.

"We need to get out of this corridor," Sarah yelled. "It's getting too dangerous in here!"

"No argument from me on that one!" Lee snapped.

Walt tapped the comm. of his helmet. "Cally, can you navigate us out of here?"

Cally was the team's tech and engineer. She hadn't entered the installation with them. Walt pictured her reclining in her seat at the sensor/comm. console in the rear of their armored personnel carrier, the Beast. She had a rougher time earning the points needed to level up than the rest of them did, almost always staying behind, but if the team didn't have someone playing the type of character that she was, they would have all been dead a long time ago.

"You're almost there already, boss man," Cally's voice answered him. "Take the second door around the bend in the corridor you're heading down."

"This way!" Walt told the others as he raced through them, continuing on along the corridor.

Sarah and Lee were hot on his heels as Walt's boots skidded on the metal floor, taking the bend in the corridor that led to where Cally had told him to go. Brent had held back to further slow down the pack of the dead that were still after them. Walt heard Brent's heavy shotgun thunder three times in rapid succession.

Walt held up a hand, gesturing for the others to stop as he spotted the door Cally had told him about. Lee, being Lee, plowed into his back. Walt grunted from the impact as he was knocked a couple of steps forward.

"What the heck?" Walt yelled at Lee as he caught himself and regained his balance.

"Sorry, man," Lee chuckled. "It's not like I got you killed or anything."

"Not this time," Sarah muttered under her breath, glaring at Lee.

Walt grabbed Lee by the front of his uniform and pulled him close.

"Get it together," Walt raged. "We're almost done with this level and none of us need you fragging it up. Got it?"

Lee at least looked serious and sincere when he answered, "Yes, sir."

Brent rounded the bend in the corridor joining them. He took one look at Walt and Lee and growled, "We got company coming!"

"Cally, what's on the other side of this door?" Walt demanded. "Does it lead straight out of this complex?"

"It does and the path is clear," Cally answered. "Simon has made sure of that."

Simon was the team's sniper. Usually, he accompanied them, but this time, Walt had asked him to hang back and keep an eye on Cally. Walt hadn't wanted to leave her alone on this op. Though the bulk of the zombies were inside the complex, the woods surrounding it were crawling with the things as well. Besides, having back up on standby on an op. like this was always a good idea.

"The lady outside says we're good to go, guys," Walt told the others and threw open the door.

The sky was dark outside. There were no stars. Thick clouds obscured their light. A steady rain was falling and the earth of the complex's yard had been turned into wet mud. Walt stepped out into the rain, relishing the feel of it on his cheeks as he looked upwards at the sky. When he looked down across the yard towards where the Beast was parked, he saw the dozens of bodies strewn about in his path and cursed himself for not being more careful as he nearly tripped over one of them. Simon had been busy making sure they had their way out.

In the distance, he could see the glint of the lens at the end of the sniper's scope where he knelt on top of the Beast. Simon likely hadn't earned as many points as they had during their time inside the complex setting the bomb for remote detonation near its power source, but he had certainly gotten some. The amount of truly dead corpses everywhere testified to that.

"You gonna stand there all night?" Sarah nudged him as she raced through the doorway behind him and started for the Beast.

"We gotta move, boss," Brent's deep voice rumbled as one of big man's hands gave him a shove forward. Walt shook his head to clear it and joined the others as they ran across the complex's yard.

Lee's P-90 chattered as he laid down holding fire directed at the zombies attempting to emerge from the doorway to pursue them. His shots were more controlled now and fired in short bursts rather than a continuous stream. The heads of the first two zombies to come through the door virtually exploded as the bursts slammed into them.

"Forget it, Lee!" Brent urged him. "Simon will cover us!"

As Lee lowered his gun and more zombies emerged from the doorway, one of their heads snapped back with a fist-sized bullet hole in its forehead.

"Show off," Lee muttered as he turned and ran after the rest of the group.

Walt saw the barrel of Simon's rifle flash several times as he ran but he didn't look back to see how many of the zombies had made it through the doorway now. He just kept on running, his legs pumping under him and his breath coming in ragged gasps.

The side door of the armored personnel carrier slid open. Cally was standing there with a pistol clutched in one hand and her other extended to him. Walt took it, allowing Cally to help pull him forward as the leaped into the APC.

The Beast's engine was running, but Walt could barely hear it over the hungry moans of the dead. The gunshots in the complex's yard were calling in the dead that had been lurking about in the trees. At a glance, Walt estimated there were at least five dozen of the creatures. They were spread out though and slow moving. The real danger was from the closer ones coming through the door they had left open behind them.

Brent reached the APC next, ducking his head as he climbed into it. The big man flopped into one its rear seats and went to work reloading his shotgun. Sarah and Lee were only a short distance away and coming in fast.

Walt's heart skipped a beat as he saw Lee's feet slip out from under him in the mud. The kid hit the ground hard with a pained grunt. Sarah must have heard him because she came to a stop and whirled about running towards where he lay sprawled out. Walt could see that the fall hadn't knocked him out, but the kid was having trouble getting to his feet because he was panicking.

Sarah slung her crossbow onto her back by its strap and yanked the pistol on her hip free of its holster. One of the faster dead came lunging at her, its lips parted in a snarl, as the three remaining fingers of its right hand reached for her. The dead man was missing his other arm entirely. Sarah easily dodged the grab he made at her and brought up her pistol level with his forehead, squeezing its trigger. The point-blank shot splashed gore over her. She swept the barrel of his weapon around to engage the next closest zombies, but one of them dropped before she ever fired a shot. Walt knew that was Simon's work. The sniper was still on top of the APC and covering the two of them as best as he could as Sarah sent the second zombie back to hell with a shot of her own.

"On your feet, cowboy!" Sarah screamed as she grabbed Lee, yanking him up.

"Boss!" Walt felt Cally's hand on his shoulder, directing his attention elsewhere, away from Sarah and Lee.

The zombies from the woods were beginning to reach the opposite side of the Beast. It rocked as their cold, dead hands pounded against its armor. As yet, they still weren't really a threat, but they very soon could be if enough of them gathered to roll the vehicle over.

Walt raised his AK-47 to brace it against his shoulder and fired a three-round burst into the chest of a zombie that had gotten a little too close to Sarah and Lee as they ran. The zombie staggered backwards as its ribcage was punched inward. Walt didn't bother following up with a headshot. Sarah and Lee were clear of the thing's reach and that was all that mattered. The two of them reached the APC. Sarah shoved Lee inside first and followed after him. Walt, lowering his weapon, slammed the door behind them.

"Cally!" Walt barked at the team's tech.

"Hold on!" Cally warned as she kicked the Beast into gear. The APC lurched forward, plowing through and rolling over the dead creatures clustered in front of it. It bounced as its wheels crushed their bodies beneath it.

"It's time," Brent said from where he sat in the APC's rear.

"Indeed it is." Walt smiled, removing the remote detonator from the pocket of his uniform. His thumb squeezed down its activation button.

The complex that had given birth to the zombie virus blew as the Beast sped away from it. Pieces of the building spun upwards into the air as it blossomed into a raging fireball that lit the night.

Level 1 completed! boomed the voice of the game controlling A.I.

The Beast and everyone aboard it blinked out of existence. They respawned in the Hub where the team was given the opportunity to re-gear up and trade out equipment before the next level of the game began. The Hub was a vast place that resembled the interior of a military warehouse with a small comm. section midway along its right side wall. The team poured out of the Beast.

"Well, that was a lot easier than I thought it was going to be," Simon said, laughing.

Covered in mud and gore, Sarah shot him a glare. She activated her avatar control mod. that she wore on her wrist. The invisible bracelet shimmered into sight. Typing a command into it, her tattered and filth-smeared uniform changed into a clean one.

The rest of the team was busy cleaning themselves up too and checking their weapons into storage. No one knew exactly what they were going to need for the next mission yet. It was easier and faster to dump everything and then pick up what you needed than to try to just swap out singular items.

Walt was already at the Hub's comm. console, checking into what their next "mission" was going to be. Cally joined him there.

"Walt, I know my class isn't really geared towards combat, but it's boring just sitting around in the Beast all the time," she said.

"Cally, you're the one that picked your class, not me, and frankly, we need you to play it. Someone has to or we'd be moving around blind out there on nearly every level," Walt pointed out. "You've never minded doing it before."

"I know, Walt." Cally shrugged. "I'm just so close to leveling up and one op. in the field outside the Beast would get me there."

Walt grinned at her. "So that's what this is really about."

"You guys are all Level 4s and I am still stuck at level 2," Cally replied. "I just don't want to be left completely behind, you know?"

"I get it," Walt assured her. "Let's see what's up next and we can talk about then, okay?"

"Okay," Cally agreed reluctantly.

Walt sat down at the comm. console with Cally looking over his shoulder at its screen.

"Looks like we've a choice," Walt said. "Werewolves or ghosts."

Lee, having heard them, came bounding over. "Werewolves, man! Ghosts suck! You can't shoot the bastards without special gear that costs a fortune!"

"Regretting spending so much on that P-90 now, are we?" Walt said, smirking. Every weapon in the game had a "cash" point value. One earned those points just like they did experience points, only cash points were harder to obtain. One always hoped to get better gear through item drops rather than being forced to buy it, but if you desperately wanted a specific weapon, sometimes buying it was the only sure means of getting it.

"Frag you, boss man." Lee shot him a bird.

"Watch it, Lee," Walt growled.

Brent came sauntering over to the comm. console. "So what are we after next, Walt?"

Sarah and Simon joined them, waiting like Brent, to hear Walt's answer.

"Ghosts or werewolves," Cally answered for him.

"Team vote?" Sarah suggested.

"Hold on," Walt ordered. "Cally wants to be in the field on this next op. We need to consider that as we're deciding."

"What? Really?" Brent stared at Cally.

"Really," she shot back at him.

"Ghosts drain levels and totally suck to go up against," Lee said. "Werewolves are a straight forward, fun shoot'em up. I mean, come on, guys!"

"I'm with Lee," Simon agreed. "If I wanted to hunt ghosts, I'd be playing a different game."

"Yeah," Sarah answered. "Werewolves sound a lot more fun."

"But what about Cally?" Brent asked. "We can't afford to lose her."

"Worst case, she dies and loses a level of experience," Lee pointed out. "There's just as much of a chance of that happening if we go up against ghosts. One touch from those things and BAM!"

"Hey! I'm standing right here!" Cally reminded the others.

"I say we leave it up to Cally," Walt suggested. "Anyone got a problem with that?"

Lee started to speak up.

"Except you, Lee!" Walt cut him off.

"Fine by me," Sarah answered.

"Cally's call," Simon agreed.

"I just want her to be safe," Brent said.

Walt looked over at Cally. "It's your call then and your butt on the line. I'm sure we'll all do what we can to look out for you but …"

"Werewolves," she answered before he could even finish what he was trying to say.

"Werewolves it is then," Walt replied. "Everyone gear up. Let's be out of the Hub and back in the field in five!"

****

The team gathered back aboard the Beast. Brent, Lee, and Sarah sat in the Beast's rear compartment, checking their weapons. Cally was at the APC's sensor station. Walt was in the driver's seat with Simon beside him. The Beast was a custom-built APC. She was tough, fast, and tricked out with Sci-Fi level systems. The Beast weighed close to 17 tons and was based on the U.S.-made Stryker. She was taller than the Stryker though and featured a left-side sliding door in addition to her rear one. A remote-controlled machine gun was mounted on her top. The addition of the high-tech sensor station in the middle of her interior reduced her internal space, but there was still plenty of room for the team of six and their equipment. Her maximum speed in optimal conditions topped out at around one hundred and ten miles per hour. While a Stryker's engine was three hundred and fifty horsepower, the Beast's was able to generate four hundred, making her truly worthy of the nickname given to her by the team.

Walt glanced over at Simon. "You ready to go hunting?"

"You know it," the team's sniper said, grinning at him.

Walt turned the Beast's ignition switch and her engine roared to life. The door that led out of the Hub rose upwards and Walt drove her through it.

Level 2 commencing! Objective - Find and eliminate all members of werewolf family, the voice of the game's A.I. boomed, seeming to come from everywhere at once as the world flashed and the Beast materialized bouncing along a curvy, gravel road. Thick trees lined the roadside and the moon was high and bright in the sky above.

Walt slowed the Beast to a cautious pace. "Cally?"

"Running a sensor sweep of the woods now, boss," she answered him.

"You ever see that movie with the squad of soldiers fighting werewolves?" Simon asked.

"Not much of a horror fan," Walt replied with a grunt. "At least not when it comes to movies."

"What?" Simon asked, sounding utterly shocked.

"I'm more of a book guy," Walt explained. "King, Lovecraft, Shelley …"

"Somehow that makes sense when you say it," Simon commented. "Explains how you know so much that some of the rest of us don't."

"Picking up lifeforms in the woods, Walt!" Cally cut in. "I've got three so far and possibly a fourth."

"Locations?" Walt asked.

"Wait!" Simon protested. "What do you mean maybe a fourth?"

"Something is messing with the Beast's sensors. I can't get a clear reading on the fourth one," Cally responded.

"Cally, just tell us about the three you're sure of," Walt ordered. "Where are they?"

Walt took his eyes from the road ahead of him for a moment to glance over his shoulder at Cally where she sat at the sensor station.

"Two of them are coming down the hill to the Beast's right; the other is headed towards us from the left. They're … They're CBDR," she exclaimed.

"What the heck does that mean?" Simon griped.

"Naval jargon, I think. It means constant bearing, decreasing range," Walt told him. "But that doesn't make any sense. We're supposed to be hunting them down. They're not supposed to be coming for us!"

"Hey! I ain't complaining," Simon laughed. "If they want to come to us and make this level easier, that's fine by me."

"No." Walt shook his head. "It's not right. Something's wrong here."

A creature that could only be a werewolf came leaping out of the trees at the Beast on its right side. The werewolf's body slammed into the APC with enough force to nearly cause Walt to lose control of the vehicle despite its cautious speed. The Beast veered to the left from the werewolf's impact. Walt heard the monster scampering up the Beast's side, its claws raking over and digging into her armor as it moved upwards.

"It's got to be going for the gun up there!" Simon yelled. "It must be trying to take it out."

"Blow it to pieces!" Walt ordered.

Simon activated the remote-controlled weapon. It began to swivel around in the direction that the werewolf was approaching it from. Its barrel was already blazing as it spat out a stream of continuous high-caliber rounds. Simon was watching through the gun's optics, hoping to see the splattering head of werewolf. What he saw though was hair-covered fingers reach in from the gun's right to clasp its barrel. The barrel bent under the pressure those fingers exerted on it. The barrel blew as Simon's screen went black.

"Holy crap!" Simon shouted. "That thing is fast."

"Incoming!" Cally yelled from the sensor station. "Three o'clock!"

Another werewolf emerged from the trees. It was moving so fast it seemed to blur as it sped towards the Beast. Walt had no chance to try to swerve from its path before the monster struck the APC. It rammed directly into the left-side tires, bouncing the Beast's wheels up from the road as it shattered their axle. The Beast whined forward a few more yards and came to a grinding halt.

"You believing me that something's wrong here yet?" Walt barked at Simon as both he and the sniper popped their seatbelts and headed for the Beast's rear.

"Did those things really just stop the Beast?" Sarah said, looking shaken by the thought.

"Everybody out!" Walt ordered. "We're gonna have to engage these mothers here, right now, and take them out before more show up! Cally, I'm sorry, but you need to hang back on this one!"

"Bugger that!" Cally yelled, grabbing up the Kriss Vector SMG she had chosen for the op.

"On my mark," Brent said as he aimed the barrels of his double-barreled, automatic shotgun at the interior side of the Beast's side door. If one of the werewolves was waiting on the other side of it when Sarah slid it open, the mother was going to be sorry. It was.

The side door slid open. The werewolf waiting there was met by the thunderous roar of Brent's automatic shotgun. The blasts tore its upper body to bloody shreds in an explosion of gore and blood. Since all of the team's weapons were loaded up with silver rounds, the thing wouldn't be regenerating either.

Sarah was through the door first. She had traded her crossbow for a TAR-21. Walt followed her out, carrying his custom-made AK-47. The two of them had barely cleared the door when the next wolf came at them. This one had shifted its form to that of a giant wolf and moved on four legs. Its mouth snarled at them as it sprang at Sarah. Sarah threw herself sideways, dodging the beast's attack as Walt whipped up the barrel of his rifle and blew ragged holes in the wolf's side, knocking it to the ground. The wolf lay there twitching as the poison of the silver bullets inside its body did its work.

Cally was next out of the Beast with Brent on her heels. The last of the three wolves that had brought the Beast to a halt came bounding across its roof to come at Brent from above and behind. Brent spun to meet it too late. One of its clawed hands slapped his automatic shotgun from the big man's grasp as it plowed into him, taking them both to the road. Only Brent's combat armor saved him from the wolf's claws as they raked across his shoulder as he tried to fight his way out from under the creature. The claws tore ragged grooves in his armor but didn't reach his skin.

"Brent!" Cally screamed, unable to get a clear shot at the wolf with her SMG.

Straining with every muscle in his massive frame, Brent heaved the wolf off of him and flung it several feet from where he lay. The wolf was back on its feet in less than a heartbeat, rage burning in its yellow eyes.

"Hey!" Lee called at the monster as he emerged from the Beast.

The werewolf's head snapped around in his direction just as Lee opened fire with his P-90. Lee missed the head shot he had been going for, but his bullets dug into the monster's throat, shoulders, and upper chest. The werewolf tried to shriek in pain, but the noise that came out of it more closely resembled the gurgle of a drowning man as its own blood ran down its throat. It flopped over onto the road and didn't move again.

"Clear!" Simon shouted. He had been the last out of the Beast and moved around it to scope out the woods on the APC's other side. "For now, anyway."

"This is totally fragged up!" Walt shouted. "They're not supposed to be coming after us."

"But they are," Sarah pointed out, "and you can bet the rest of this pack is on their way to us right now."

Howls rang out in the distant trees from every direction. Walt couldn't be sure but he thought he counted eight distinct voices among them.

"We can't stay here," Simon advised. "We're too exposed like this. As fast as those things are …"

"Right," Walt agreed, pulling himself together. No matter how strange things were with this level so far, they were still playing it, and there was no pause button in this kind of game. "Cally?"

"There's a house a few klicks from here to the west," Cally said, taking a look at her handheld. It was tied into the Beast's sensors.

"That means cutting through the woods if we're going to try to get there fast," Simon warned.

"Nothing for it," Walt replied with a sigh. "Sarah, Lee, take point. Cally, I want you in the middle. Brent, you've got the rear."

"Roger that," Brent answered.

The team moved out, leaving the Beast behind. They all knew they would have to return to it when the op. was complete, but for now, the house Cally was navigating them to was their safest bet. Walt just hoped the place would be as defensible as they were all hoping it would be.

The night was dark, but the full moon above was bright and cast long shadows throughout the woods. It gave off more than enough light to keep them from being forced to use their lowlight optics. There was a chill in the air as the wind drifted through the trees, causing their branches to sway. The distant howls were drawing closer so Walt ordered the team to pick up their pace.

"There it is!" Lee said as the team emerged into the small clearing around the house.

It was a two-story structure and that looked abandoned. Thick vines grew up its sides and some of its upstairs windows appeared to be shattered. The door looked intact though. Walt raced passed Lee and Sarah to see if it was locked. They covered him as the rest of the team spread out, facing the trees with their weapons trained on them.

Walt tried the doorknob. The door opened at his touch, creaking inward on its rusty hinges.

"That's so cliché,'" Cally complained.

Lee chuckled at her comment.

The team made a quick sweep of the house. It was as vacant as it looked to be. The floors and furniture were covered in dust. There was a kitchen, a living room, a bath, single bedroom downstairs, and another bath and two more bedrooms upstairs.

"Simon, I want you upstairs watching for company," Walt ordered.

"On it," Simon said, racing up the stairs, his sniper rifle in hand.

"Lee, go with him and watch his back," Walt said. "Cally, I want you up there too. It's likely going to be a lot safer than being down here when the wolves show."

Cally didn't argue this time. She followed Simon and Lee up.

"Brent, you got the door." Walt had locked it once the team had all made it inside, but he knew it wouldn't even really slow the wolves down when they arrived.

"I got the back door," Sarah said before Walt could say anything else and took off towards the kitchen.

Walt crept over to the living room window and stood there staring out at the trees. It was just a matter of time until the wolves arrived now. He hoped they were all ready.

The wait was a short one. The wolves came bursting from the trees in a mad charge for the house. Walt counted five of them coming towards the front of the house which meant either he was wrong about how many of the monsters were out there or Sarah was about to have her hands full at the house's rear.

Brent held his fire, waiting on the wolves to tear through the door he was guarding, but Simon opened up on the monsters from an upstairs window. His rifle cracked and a wolf dropped, a hole blown through its forehead. Lee's P-90 chattered in the wake of Simon's first shot. Walt joined in, knocking out the living room with the butt of his AK-4 and then spun the weapon around to brace it against his shoulder. It kicked against him as he squeezed its trigger tight. Spent shell casings clattered to the floor at his feet and hosed an approaching werewolf with a blast of fully automatic fire. The werewolf howled in pain as it staggered and lost its stride. It didn't fall though. Its yellow eyes burnt brighter in the moonlight and it seemed determined to reach him no matter how much damage he inflicted on it.

Sarah had taken a position well away from the house's rear door in the kitchen and she was glad she had. The door exploded inward in a shower of splinters as a hulking nine foot tall werewolf came crashing through it at her. She leveled the barrel of her TAR-21 at the beast and let the monster have it. Bullets raked the monster's wide chest, tearing chunks of flesh and fur from it. It wasn't enough to stop the werewolf, but it did royally tick the thing off. The werewolf roared, lunging to grab the barrel of her TAR-21. Its fingers closed around it and bent it upward. Sarah let go of the gun, falling back, as she drew a set of matching revolvers from the holsters on her hips with blinding speed. The werewolf flung the broken SMG aside as it showed her its teeth in a fierce, hungry snarl. Sarah's thumbs worked the hammers of her revolvers as they thundered in rapid succession. Her first shot blew a chunk of meat from the werewolf's right shoulder. Her second clipped the beast's throat, causing it to raise a hand to cover the wound the bullet had left there. Blood spurted from the wound as her third shot entered the monster's right cheek. It spat teeth and blood, reeling from the barrage of fire she continued to pour into it. Her fourth shot thudded into the monster's sternum. The werewolf grunted from the impact. Sarah put three more bullets into the werewolf before she leaped through the kitchen door leading to the living room. She would have liked to have stayed and finished the werewolf, but a second monster, just as large and deadly as it was, had entered the kitchen behind it. As good as she was with her revolvers, they simply didn't give her the firepower to go up against two of the werewolves at once.

Walt threw himself sideways as the werewolf he had poured fire into reached the living room window and came bounding through it. It landed on the floor behind him, knocking over an end table near the room's couch in the process. The beast kicked the table at Walt as he was trying to regain his balance. The table smashed into him, knocking the air from his lungs as it shattered against the combat armor covering his chest. Brent spun in his position at the house's front door to engage the beast. His automatic shotgun blazed, spitting a three-round burst at the werewolf. The werewolf jumped up, clinging to the ceiling by its claws as Brent's devastating blast of fire ripped apart the wall behind where it had stood. The werewolf swung itself towards Brent and thudded onto the floor in front of him, taking a swipe at him with it claws. Brent reeled away from the attack as Sarah appeared from the kitchen, her revolvers cracking twice as the werewolf's eyes were reduced to pulp inside their sockets as her shots tore into them. The werewolf's hands reached up to cover what was left of its mangled eyes as it squealed in pain. Brent finished the monster, emptying the rest of his shotgun's magazine into it at close to point-blank range, nearly cutting the werewolf in half along the center of its body. The thing's intestines spilled out of it, blood-slicked, purple strands that wrapped about its flailing legs before the monster collapsed to the floor.

One of the werewolves approaching the house kicked against the ground with its powerful legs and soared upwards through the night at Simon's position on the second floor. The sniper hurled himself from the beast's path as its heavy form caved in the wall around the window he had been firing through. Simon had shoved Lee in the opposite direction as he dodged the beast. Lee, taken off guard, had ended up landing on his butt. The beast was only a few feet from both of them as it rose up from the crouch it had landed in. It made no move towards them. The monster's yellow eyes had fallen on Cally who stood at the bedroom's far wall near the door leading out of it.

"Guys! Help!" Cally screamed as the werewolf surged forward at her. Her trembling, fumbling hands tried to bring her Vector SMG up at the beast but it reached her, yanking the weapon from her grasp before she could get off a single shot. The werewolf used the stolen weapon like a club smashing it into Cally's face. The blow sent her careening against the room's wall. The werewolf turned as Lee came charging it in an attempt to save Cally. Giving a pleasure-filled huff, the werewolf rammed the Vector through Lee. The gun impaled him as his own weapon clanged onto the room's floor and his hands clutched the part of the weapon that was still outside of his guts. The werewolf effortlessly lifted him on the weapon, causing him to slide along the small bit that wasn't in him or had passed through him already. Lee's body twitched as the werewolf held him in the air, watching him die as his eyes rolled up to show only whites.

"Lee!" Simon yelled, back on his feet.

The werewolf tossed Lee's corpse at the sniper. Simon grunted as his dead friend's body slammed into him, knocking him back over and sending his rifle bouncing across the room. Rearing its head towards the ceiling, the werewolf gave a howl of triumph.

Cally fought to stay conscious as the world spun before her eyes and she tasted the salty iron of her own blood in her mouth. Her legs kicked against the wood of the floor, shoving her farther away from where the werewolf stood. Fingers clawing at the butt of the pistol holstered on her belt, she finally got the weapon free. Cally raised it in her trembling hands. The werewolf seemed totally unconcerned by the gun as it moved to tower over her. As it leaned over to reach for her, tears of fear and desperation ran over the curves of Cally's cheeks. She squeezed the pistol's trigger. The barrel of the pistol flashed as a hole blossomed in the palm of the werewolf's reaching hand. The monster jerked its injured hand away and snarled loudly as Cally rolled under the room's bed. Grabbing the bed, the werewolf flipped it over, uncovering her and exposing her to its fury. Cally figured she was dead.

The werewolf's chest exploded above her, raining showers of gore onto her.

"That one was for Lee, you bastard," Cally heard Simon shout.

She barely managed to escape the werewolf's collapsing heavy body as it fell over. Cally scrambled to her feet, her pistol still clutched in a white-knuckled hold in her hand. The next thing she knew, Simon was beside her, his hand holding the underside of her chin as he looked over the wreckage that was her face.

"You okay?" the sniper asked.

Cally didn't dare to try to talk with her nose broken and her lips bashed and nearly swollen shut so just nodded.

"This isn't over yet," Simon warned her as they heard the continuous bursts of gunfire from downstairs. "We've got to help the others."

Cally gestured at Lee's body. Simon shook his head.

"He's dead. We've got to leave him," he told her. "He should respawn soon anyway."

Downstairs, Walt, Brent, and Sarah were in the fight of their lives. Three of the werewolves who had entered the house to engage them were dead now but unfortunately, that meant there were three more still alive and very angry. Sarah's expression was grim as she quickly reloaded her revolvers and ran for her life towards the stairs leading upstairs with one of the monsters on her heels. Another of the werewolves wrestled with Brent near the house's now shattered front door. The monster had come bursting through it and caught the big man off guard. The fingers of its hands were wrapped around Brent's shotgun, but the giant refused to let the weapon go. Walt ducked the swiping claws of the third werewolf as it tried to remove his head from his shoulders.

Her revolvers reloaded and halfway up the stairs, Sarah spun about to suddenly confront the werewolf chasing her. The monster looked at her with wide, surprised eyes in the moment before the barrels of her pistols touched its forehead and she pulled the triggers. Brain matter and bone fragments exited the backside of the monster's skull in an explosion of blood. Sarah lashed out with one of her boots even as the werewolf started to fall, kicking it and sending its corpse crashing down the stairs. A feral grin parted her lips as she whirled about to shoot at the werewolf wrestling with Brent. Her bullets peppered its back with ragged holes, forcing the monster to let go of the big man. Brent seized the moment, ripping his shotgun away from the creature's grasp. He shoved its barrel into the werewolf's gut and tried to blow the monster to hell. The shotgun clicked empty instead.

Walt dropped to the living room floor, rolling across it to come up behind its overturned couch. He fired a burst from his AK-47 at the werewolf chasing him as he did so. The burst caught the monster in its chest, spraying blood into the air. The creature made the fatal mistake of pausing to look down at its wounds, giving Walt the chance to end it. Walt emptied his AK-47 into the hulking beast. Its body jerked about as a steam of high-velocity silver bullets sent it back to whatever hell it had crawled out of.

The werewolf fighting Brent lifted the big man and flung him across the living room. He thudded into its far wall with the sound of breaking bones. Brent slumped where he fell at the bottom of the wall unconscious as the werewolf moved in for the kill.

Sarah's pistols clicked empty again but before she could move to try to reload them, Simon appeared next to her, shoving her out of the way so he could get a shot at the monster going for Brent. The sniper braced his rifle against his shoulder, aiming with almost impossible speed, and took his shot. It was a move only someone that had maxed out their character's targeting ability could pull off. His bullet severed the werewolf's spine at the base of its neck. The monster gave a pained cry and toppled to rest on the floor. It was whining as Walt walked calmly over to it, reloading his AK-47 as he went. Walt lowered the AK-47's barrel to touch the werewolf's forehead and put the monster out of its misery with a single burst.

"Where in the holy Hades is Lee?" Walt snapped, jerking his head up to look at Sarah and Simon on the stairs. Cally stood a few steps above them at the top of the stairs. She appeared to be barely standing. Her face was a wreck of gore. Walt flinched in sympathetic pain at the sight of it. A twinge of guilt stung him for letting her come along instead of hanging back in the Beast on this one. Of course, if he had left her there on *this* level, as screwed up as it was, she might be dead.

"Didn't he respawn down here?" Simon asked, his gaze scanning over the room below in search of the kid.

"Haven't seen any sign of him," Walt said. "I'll say it again, something is really fragging messed up with this level."

"Walt," Brent called to him. "There's another wolf outside in the yard."

Walt turned to look out the shattered main window. In the night stood a *thing* that resembled a werewolf but emanated the power of something far greater. Its eyes burned a glowing red in the light of the full moon like miniature suns blazing in their sockets. Walt knew werewolves were supposed to be *big* but this sucker stood nearly twelve feet tall. Muscles rippled beneath the fur covering its body as it moved and took a step towards the house.

"You have killed my children," the beast roared in a voice that shook the very walls around Walt and the others.

"You bet your ass we did!" Sarah shouted at the monster. "Come on in and let's see what happens to you."

The werewolf-thing laughed at her crude threat.

"You are all little more than children yourselves," it said softly. "That will not spare you from the master's mercy. You have been chosen and whether at my hands or no, you *will* all die."

"Oh come on," Brent growled, frustrated. "Let's get this level over with."

The big man tugged his spare shotgun from where it was holstered on his back and chunked its initial round into its chamber.

"Wait!" Walt shouted wanting to hear more of what the werewolf-thing had to say but it was too late. Brent opened fire and the battle was joined.

Brent emptied the automatic shotgun's entire magazine at the creature in one continuous booming of thunder. Not a single slug struck the monster though. The slugs slashed through the air where it had been standing as it moved so fast it almost blurred, charging towards the house's shattered window and the living room behind it where the team had gathered.

Walt knew Sarah's character had a speed score almost equal to Simon's targeting ability, but even as fast as she brought up her pistols, it wasn't fast enough. The werewolf plunged through the window into the ranks of the team and batted her from its path. Sarah went flying across the room to smack into its left wall. The wall cracked at the spot where the bulk of her body slammed into it. Sarah flopped away from it to land sprawled out and unconscious on the floor.

Unbelievably, it was Cally who drew first blood against the monster. Her pistol bucked in the two-handed grip she held it in as she put a trio of silver rounds into the monster's side as it whirled about at Brent who was the next closest to it. Brent blocked its slashing claws with his shotgun. The weapon snapped apart along its middle from the force of the monster's strike. Jumping back away from the werewolf-thing, Brent drew a large, silver-bladed knife from his boot. With both his shotguns gone, it was the only weapon he had left.

Walt drew the monster's attention as he poured fire into its back. Bullets ripped a jagged path from just above its buttocks to the base of its neck. The werewolf-thing growled against the pain it had to be feeling as it spun again to engage him. Not a single one of them stood a chance against this thing alone and Walt knew it. They were going to have to work together to bring it down. He just hoped that with Lee missing and Sarah out of the fight that they were up to the task. There wasn't supposed to be *anything* higher than a level 5 in this part of the game, PC or NPC, yet this thing was clearly higher in level.

Brent threw his knife. It spun end over end through the air towards the werewolf-thing. The monster caught the knife and hurled it at Cally. Simon tackled her, taking her to the floor as the knife thunked into the wall above them.

Reloading his rifle on the move, Walt tried to come up with a plan for how to deal with the monster. Sadly, he couldn't think of a blasted thing. The best they could hope for was to stay alive long enough to wear it down and that wasn't looking very likely at the moment. The monster was on his heels and overtaking him. He felt a clawed and hairy hand grab him around the neck from behind. Walt was lifted from the floor and thrown into the railing of the stairs leading upstairs. His body crashed through them to thud onto the stairs. Splinters pierced his gloves from where he had tried to soften his landing. Blood seeped from his hands and his AK-47 lay several feet from where he had landed. He smelt the foul stench of the monster's breath as he looked up into its burning red eyes and knew he was dead.

Simon's rifle cracked. A carefully aimed bullet blew through the werewolf-thing's skull, spraying gore over Walt. The monster jerked its head up, one of its fingers probing its now empty left eye socket.

"Die, you mother!" Simon yelled as he took another shot at the monster.

Walt scrambled to retrieve his rifle as the monster went after Simon. He ignored the pain in his hands as he grasped the weapon and yanked it up from where it rested on the stairs below him. He aimed the weapon at monster's back. His fingers moved to the trigger of the GP-25 grenade launcher mounted on the underside of its barrel. This was going to hurt.

Firing the grenade at point-blank range into the monster's back, Walt threw himself sideways as he took the shot. The grenade struck the monster like a bullet sinking into the meat of its lower back and exploded there. The concussive shockwave of the blast slammed into Walt as the monster blew apart.

Walt felt Simon's hand slapping his head from one side to the other.

"Wake up, Walt!" the sniper was screaming at him.

The world slowly came into focus as Walt opened his eyes. He felt as if he had been run over by an eighteen wheeler. His whole body ached. He felt Simon pulling him to his feet.

"We have to get back to the Beast," he heard Simon telling the others.

As Simon held him and helped keep him on his feet, Walt looked around at the others. They were all battered and exhausted. The team had never taken a beating as bad as this one before. Whatever was screwed up with this level, it had caught them with their pants around their ankles and they had paid the price for it.

"Can you move, Walt?" Simon asked.

Walt nodded, not able to form words yet.

Brent was carrying Sarah. The gunslinger was still unconscious. And poor Cally …Walt couldn't even imagine the amount of pain she had to be in from her mangled face and broken nose. The young tech was keeping it together though.

As the team left the house and walked along the road to where the Beast was waiting for them, Simon said, "That was one heck of a risky move, Walt. I can't believe you had the stones to try it."

"No other choice," Walt managed to get out.

"There's still no sign of Lee," Simon told him. "He hasn't respawned anywhere according to Cally."

That made even less sense than the higher than level 5 monster that shouldn't have been on this level to Walt. When you died in the game, you always came back. That was just how it worked. You might lose some experience points or an item or two but you always respawned. It was a fundamental rule.

The team reached the Beast. Brent laid Sarah down gently on one of its rear seats as Simon helped Walt into the APC. Cally was clearly in a hurry to get back to the Hub because she headed straight for the driver's seat and fired up the Beast's engine. The

APC had taken some damage too but it didn't really need to move. Its motor turning over and roaring to life was enough to signal the game that the team was done with the level and headed home. The Beast blinked out of existence as the level ended.

The Beast and the team with it re-materialized inside the warehouse-like structure of the game's central Hub. The transition healed their wounds in the process. Walt felt the healing energy flowing through him and watched as the wounds on his hands closed themselves. Cally let out a shriek of glee as her fingers reached up to rub at her newly healed face and nose.

Sarah came to and sat up on the seat she had been sprawled out on. "What in the devil just happened?"

"I don't have a fracking clue." Simon shook his head. "But Walt was right. That level was truly fragged up."

Walt sprang up from his seat, shoving Simon out of his way as he ran to open the Beast's side door and leap out into the Hub.

"Lee!" Walt screamed as his eyes searched for the kid. Surely he had to have respawned here since he hadn't re-entered the level they had just fought through.

There was no sign of Lee anywhere to be found in the Hub.

"Lee isn't here?" Brent asked in disbelief.

Walt shook his head.

"Then where in the heck is he?" Sarah growled as she emerged from the Beast.

"I don't know," Walt replied, frowning, "but we need to find out. Cally, you have any idea on how to do that?"

"Well, we could check his up-link," Cally suggested. "Maybe he logged out of the game when he died."

"Do it," Walt ordered her.

Walt and the others followed her to the Hub's central console as she slid into the seat in front of it. Cally's fingers danced over the keys of its controls as she brought the system online.

An image of Lee in the real world filled the console's screen. Everyone stared at Lee's limp and slumped-over body where it sat on a couch in what appeared to be his living room. The total immersion helmet covered the upper half of Lee's head. Blood leaked from beneath it where his eyes were covered by it and more blood seeped from the corner of his mouth like drool.

"Lee ... Lee's dead," Cally muttered weakly.

"What the hell do you mean he's dead?" Brent growled. "That's impossible."

"That's him in the real world." Cally stabbed a finger at the console's screen. "Don't you see? Look at him. His vitals say he's dead too."

"But you just said that we are looking at him in the real world," Sarah pointed out.

"We are," Cally confirmed. "When he died here, he died there too."

"You're telling us that the kid couldn't handle the game, had some kind of seizure, and died out there in the real world?" Simon challenged her. "That's messed up. Tough break for him."

"Simon!" Sarah raged. "Not even you can be that heartless. Come on! Lee is dead. I mean really dead and you're not even taking it seriously."

"That's not what I said, Simon," Cally spoke up. "I think the game killed him."

"The game can't kill anyone," Brent pointed out. "There are too many safety features in the programming and the interface helmets for that to happen."

"I didn't say I could explain it." Cally looked up at Brent as the big man towered over her. "But I really think that's what happened."

"We can't help Lee," Walt said sadly. "We don't even know for sure what's happened to him. The question now is, do we keep playing or log out ourselves?"

"Lee would have wanted us to go on," Sarah said. "Besides, he couldn't really be dead, could he?"

Brent nodded. "I agree with the going on part. It's not often that all of us get to log in together. We're a good team and I really think we can beat this game. We might even end up getting one of the better ranks worldwide if we really focus and do our best."

"Whatever happened to Lee has to be a fluke." Simon turned to Walt. "And Brent's right. We logged in to win, so let's do it for Lee. No matter how it might look, we don't know that he's dead out there. It's much more likely the kid just had a seizure or something."

"Cally?" Walt asked.

"I'm part of this team, Walt. Everyone else seems to want to keep playing and you guys are going to need your tech with you," Cally answered. "I'll do it for Lee. I do think we need to try contact someone out there in the real world and let them know about Lee though."

"No point," Simon cut in. "You can bet the game already has. It's designed to do that in the event of an accident. Not to mention, Lee's just a kid. His parents will find him and get him help if he needs it. I mean, we don't really know for sure that he's dead no matter what it looks like."

"Okay, we're all agreed then. The game goes on," Walt said, taking comfort in Simon's words. "Let's take a look at Level 3 and find out what we're up against next."

Cally typed some commands into the control console and the image of Lee slumped over on the couch in his living room disappeared from the screen. The image of Lee was replaced by the images of a mummy on one side of the screen and an image of winged gargoyle creatures on the other.

"Looks like we have a choice again," Cally told the others as she scanned the write-up about the monsters. "The mummy track is much more focused on the roleplaying side of things. The gargoyles look to be mostly flat-out combat like the werewolves."

"I still don't understand why the werewolves came after us when we were supposed to be hunting them," Walt commented. "And that boss … That was totally creepy. Who or what is the master he was talking about it?"

Cally shrugged. "The game doesn't say anything about a master controlling the other monsters. At least I haven't been able to find anything about it in the storyline info."

"Let it go, Walt," Brent said. "What happened with those wolves had to be just a glitch."

Walt felt like the big guy was in denial about it all but didn't press him on it.

"I don't think any of us feel like roleplaying out an arc like the mummy one seems to be right now," Sarah replied. "I vote for the winged monsters."

"Me too," Simon, said moving up to put an arm around Sarah's shoulders as he spoke. She knocked it off of her, scowling at him.

"This team has always done better with combat scenarios anyway," Brent said. "I vote for the gargoyles too."

"One more vote makes it a majority for the winged monsters." Walt looked around at the others. "And I'm voting for them too. Blowing away some monsters would do us all some good."

"The gargoyles have it then." Sarah rested a comforting hand on Cally's shoulder, noticing that the girl was still struggling with Lee's death. Heck, they all were. Cally was just letting it show more.

"I got one question though." Brent tapped the image of the gargoyles on the console screen. "Are those things organic or made out of rock? I've heard of both kind and just want to be sure I load up with the right kind of firepower."

"Organic," Cally told him.

"Roger that," Brent said, flashing her a grin.

"Let's get to it then," Walt said. "Grab whatever gear you think you'll need and be back inside the Beast in five."

The team scattered to go gather their gear and use the points they had earned from the werewolves to upgrade their own abilities, leaving Walt and Cally at the control console.

"You earned enough points to level up, Cally." Walt did his best to smile.

"I know," Cally said. "Somehow, it just doesn't seem to matter as much anymore."

"Even so, you need to make your upgrades," Walt ordered her. "The team is going to need you to be the best you can out there."

Cally nodded her understanding and got up out of her seat. Walt watched her head off after the others. He stood there for a time at the control console, alone, before he went to make upgrades of his own.

It was closer to ten minutes later when all the team had finally gathered outside the Beast again. The APC's side door was open and Simon was already inside the vehicle but the others hadn't entered it yet.

"You really think this is a good idea, Walt?" Cally asked. "How do we know for sure that what happened to Lee won't happen to the next person who gets killed out there?"

"Let's just do our best to make sure that none of us get killed out there," Walt told her and then joined Simon inside the Beast. The others followed after him. Cally slid in the APC's driver's seat and fired up its engine. As the Beast drove towards the door leading out of the Hub, it faded out and then blinked back into existence, driving along the street of what looked to be a small town in America.

The town's resident had clearly fled the place, at least those that had escaped it alive. There was no sign of living people anywhere. Several buildings along the street that the Beast drove through were burning. Thick, black coils of smoke drifted towards the heavens from them. Abandoned cars and trucks made driving difficult for Cally but she didn't complain. She kept the Beast's pace slow and carefully made her way around them. Here and there corpses littered the road and the sides of the streets. From the smell of them that crept into the Beast, they had been dead for some time.

"Looks like all the NPCs are either dead or bugged out for better pastures some time ago," Sarah commented on the destruction outside the Beast.

"Figures," Brent said with a grunt. "We did pick the combat version of this level. Just be glad they're not around to get in our way and slow us down."

"Not much a sheriff in a little town like this could have done to protect it from winged monsters," Simon said.

"According to the storyline for this place, the town has been under attack every night for several days now," Cally informed them.

"It looks to be almost dusk right now," Walt said. "If we hurry, maybe we can get set up before the gargoyles show up."

"Cally …" Walt said, turning to her.

"I know, Walt," she said, meeting his eyes, "I'm staying in the Beast for this one."

"Good call." Walt smiled at her. "Everyone else, let's move!"

Sarah slid open the Beast's side door and the rest of the team spilled out into the street.

"Brent, I want you and Simon up high. Pick your spots and get to them," Walt ordered.

Simon sprinted away into the growing darkness as Brent hefted the RPG he carried and said, "You guys be careful down here."

"Count on it," Walt replied and then motioned for Brent to get going.

"Let me guess, I'm the bait," Sarah said with a grin.

"Well, you are the best looking," Walt teased her.

Sarah snorted at his compliment and then shook her head, grinning. "And just where will you be, boss?"

"Right over there." Walt pointed at the shattered window of what looked to be a general store. "I'll be ready to come out blazing when you need me," he assured her.

"You better," Sarah said.

The night wasn't as dark as it could have been. The fires crackling along the street were still in the process of burning themselves out. The smoke and the smell of the corpses were strong on the wind that blew through the street. Walt took his position behind the store's main counter, hiding himself in the shadows there as he watched Sarah outside. All they could do now was sit around and wait for the monsters to come. Walt hoped the wait would be a short one.

Sarah wandered up and down the street, trying to ignore the bodies that littered it. There weren't that many of them, truth be told, compared to some levels she had seen in the game before, but they were enough to make her uneasy. Thinking about them was the last thing she needed to be doing she reminded herself. Her eyes needed to be on the sky. The gargoyles could come swooping in from anywhere without warning. That was a favorite tactic of creatures like them in the game. Catch you by surprise and drag you up into the air where the odds were in their favor. She had opted not bring anything but her pistols and her katana for this level, figuring the less weighted down she was the better. Since the gargoyles were organic creatures and not made of rock, they should bleed just fine when she put a bullet in them.

The diner on the right side of the street looked to have blown up at some point. Debris from it was scattered about. Sarah kicked at a large dented but somehow still intact can of tomatoes. Just enough of its label remained for her to know what it was. She was getting bored of being the bait quickly and wondering if the gargoyles were ever going to make their move.

At that moment, clouds rolled by above her, blocking out the light of the moon. The night grew darker. There was still a decent enough amount of light to see by thanks to the dying fires of the randomly burning buildings. Nonetheless, Sarah paused to look up at the sky. The air felt charged with energy as if it were about to start raining. As she looked up, her eyes met the glowing green eyes of a gargoyle that was flying straight at her. Sarah's hands moved with blinding speed to draw the matching revolvers holstered on her hips. She brought them up, thumbs working their cocking hammers. There was no time to aim as she fired. Her pistols cracked, spitting lead at the monster as she threw herself to the left and rolled across the street dodging the monster's reaching hands. She knew her two shots had struck the beast as it flew over her and then darted upwards in the air to come back down landing on its feet. Bright yellow blood that seemed to glow in the night leaked from jagged holes in its chest. The gargoyle stood nine feet tall, its leathery wings spread out behind it as its lips parted in a snarl.

Sarah came up onto her feet, her revolvers cracking in rapid succession as she put six more rounds into the monster. Each entered the creature's flash with a splash of yellow blood exploding outward in its wake. The gargoyle stumbled as Sarah moved in for the kill.

Walt burst out of the store he had been hiding in, running directly towards her.

"Get down!" Walt shouted at the top of his lungs.

Sarah glanced skyward to see two more gargoyles diving from the dark clouds above on. The talons of their hands gleamed in the dim light of the fires raging along the street. As she threw herself to the asphalt, she saw the reason for Walt's warning. It wasn't just to save her from being swept up into the sky by the creatures. Brent had emerged from his cover on one of the nearby rooftops, his RPG braced and ready to fire.

The RPG launcher flashed. An instant later, one of the two descending gargoyles vanished in an explosion of heat and flames. Some of the shrapnel from the blast struck the second gargoyle as it veered hard away from the blast. The shrapnel tore at its body and wings, punching holes through them. The gargoyle careened about in the sky, trying to maintain its flight but the effort proved useless. It had been too badly hurt. The gargoyle crashed into the pavement of the street up the street from where Sarah lay.

Walt's AK-47 chattered loudly as he engaged the gargoyle Sarah had been on her way to finish before the other two had appeared. Bullets dug jagged holes in the creature's guts and lower thighs as it tried to take flight. It rose a few feet from the ground before the wounds Walt kept inflicting brought it down, hard. Walt reached its twitching body and put a final three-round burst into its skull to make sure it was dead.

"Incoming!" Simon yelled from a building across from the one that Brent was on.

Both Walt and Sarah looked up to see half a dozen more of the creatures inbound for them. There was no cover to be had in the middle of the street, nothing to keep the creatures from snatching them up to be carried into the air or tearing them apart. Sarah grunted, accepting her fate. She wasn't going out without a fight. Her pistols were nearly empty. Trying to take the time to reload was akin to suicide, so she holstered them and drew her katana, assuming a defensive stance.

Walt emptied the rest of his AK-47's magazine at the creatures. Had there been less of them, his tactic might have worked, but there were so many, so spread out, that most of his bullets missed their targets as he raked the barrel of his weapon in a wide arc, trying to do as much as damage to as many of the monsters as he could.

Sarah braced herself, sweat trickling along the curve of her back underneath her combat armor. She was ready to die as long as she managed to take one of the buggers with her. It didn't come to that though. Instead, the night lit up with the flashes of orange tracer rounds as the Beast's top-mounted, remote-controlled machine gun opened fire. Its initial blast cut four of the gargoyles to shreds, raining intestines and gore over the street below. The other gargoyles banked away from the street, trying to dodge the machine gun's second burst of fire. One of them did. The other lost a leg and part of its lower body to the burst, sending it crashing into the dancing fires of one of the still-burning buildings. The gargoyle howled and cried as it thrashed about in the flames until it finally died.

"Go Cally!" Walt shouted at the Beast, shaking his AK-47 above his head.

"It ain't over yet, boss," Walt heard Cally say over the comm. in his helmet.

"How many more?" he asked her.

"I'm picking up a dozen more hiding in the clouds up there," Cally told him.

Brent had disappeared from sight on the roof he had fired the RPG from. Walt imagined he was high-tailing it to the street to join up with them. Turning his head, Walt saw that Simon had stayed where he was.

"Twelve more!" Walt shouted at Sarah just as Brent emerged from the front door of the laundry mat he had been on the roof of.

Sarah sheathed her katana, hurrying to reload her revolvers as Brent ran up to them. The RPG was a one-shot weapon so he had discarded it and now carried his normal automatic shotgun, held at the ready.

"Wonder what they're waiting on," Brent commented.

"They're likely trying to figure out how to deal with the Beast," Walt said, laughing. "Cally must have scared the crap out of them."

"We'd be dead if it wasn't for her," Sarah told Brent.

Brent was grinning from ear to ear with pride. Sarah had never figured out if the big guy had a thing for Cally or if he saw her as if she were his little sister. The relationship between Brent and Cally was a strange one any way you looked at it, as it walked the line of being both.

"What do we do now, boss?" Brent asked. "Just stand here hoping those monsters will come to us?"

"Nothing else we can do," Walt said. "But trust me, they will. You can count on that."

Like missiles streaking from the sky, the gargoyles made their move. Two of them came diving at the Beast from its rear. The top-mounted machine gun whirred on its turret, attempting to turn and engage them. It didn't make the circle in time. The pair of gargoyles landed on the APC's roof. The one was stupid enough to move into the gun's line of fire as it reached for the weapon. The machine gun opened up, nearly vaporizing the monster at such a close range. The other gargoyle succeeded in getting a grip on the machine gun from behind it and ripped it from its turret. Sparks flew as metal whined and broke, being no match for the gargoyle's supernatural strength. The gargoyle flung the mangled weapon onto the street.

The Beast's engine roared to life. The APC lurched forward, causing the gargoyle on its roof to lose it footing. The creature caught itself mid-fall, its wings flapping rapidly to keep it aloft. Before it could adjust itself though and take off into the sky, Brent ran towards it, his automatic shotgun thundering as he went. The first slug from the weapon blew apart the gargoyle's left shoulder. The second punched into its side, flinging strands of the creature's entrails outward as the slug entered. The third finished the monster, widening the hole made by the second and nearly cutting the gargoyle in half along its middle. Its corpse thudded onto the road where the Beast had been sitting. The APC, picking up speed as it moved, raced along the street towards the edge of town.

With the Beast out of the picture and on the run, the other gargoyles joined the battle. Five of them swooped downwards from the clouds, drawing Sarah, Walt, and Brent's fire while the others landed to surround them in the street. Brent emptied his automatic shotgun into one of the creatures bearing down on them. The impact of the shotgun's slugs knocked the creature back upwards as they ripped and tore through its body. The gargoyle died instantly from Brent's barrage but that left Brent with an empty weapon. The big guy tossed it aside, yanking out his second shotgun from where it was sheathed on his back. He had just pumped its initial round into it chamber, readying it, as another gargoyle plowed into him, picking him up. Brent grunted as he felt several of ribs break and the front of his combat armor crack. The gargoyle carried him in a straight line away from the others to fling him through the front window of a diner. Glass shattered around Brent as he plunged through it and landed on the top of a table near the window. It broke beneath his weight and dumped him onto the floor. Stunned and hurting, Brent realized with a start that the diner around him was on fire. He heaved himself unto his feet just in time for a piece of what was left of its burning roof to come tumbling down on top of him. It pinned him to the floor as the flames licked at his flesh and his hair smoldered.

Walt aimed his shots carefully, making them count. His first three-round burst slammed into the forehead of one of the descending gargoyles, snapping its head back on its neck. Jerking his rifle around at the other gargoyle on a course for him, he fired again. The gargoyle swerved in the air to prevent the bullets from doing the same to it as they had its brother. Instead, they ripped a ragged line along the upper length of its left wing. The gargoyle screeched in pain but righted itself to fly over Walt, grabbing him by his arms. Walt's AK-47 was knocked from his hands in the process. The monster's wing had been injured too badly for it to follow through with its plan however. Walt's weight pulled it out of the sky and the two of them flopped onto the street together. Rolling away from the monster, Walt yanked his sidearm free of the holster on his hip. He rolled onto his back, bringing up the pistol in both hands as the gargoyle got to its feet and lunged at him. His pistol barked in rapid succession, blowing holes in the gargoyle's face and shoulders. Walt let out a sigh of relief as its corpse thudded into the street next to where he lay instead of on top of him. A puddle of blood grew around the gargoyle's body where it rested on the asphalt.

That only left one gargoyle for Sarah to deal with. It came swooping in at her, its outstretched hands ready to grab her the second she was within reach. Her katana flicked through the air as she chopped the gargoyle's hand off at the wrist and then the other, ducking under its now twisting body as it flew on over her. The gargoyle struck the asphalt head first with enough force to smash its own skull open like an overripe melon being hit by a sledgehammer.

Those five gargoyles had managed to split the team up though and the other seven creatures who were already on the ground moved in to take advantage of that fact. The Beast had made a hard turn at the end of the street and came roaring back towards the gargoyle. Its forward armor hit two of them at close to fifty miles per hour. The spine of one of the gargoyles snapped and it fell to be crushed under the wheels of the APC. The other gargoyle was dealt a glancing blow that sent it careening away from the Beast as Cally kept her foot on the gas.

Sarah and Walt found themselves facing five snarling gargoyles. One leaped at Sarah. She sidestepped its attack as the blade of her katana struck opening up its guts. Purple, blood-smeared strands spilt onto the asphalt, twisting about the creature's legs as they poured from its body. Caught up in its own entrails, the gargoyle awkwardly tried to turn and reach for her again. A second swipe of her katana took the creature's head from its shoulders to send it bouncing along the street. Walt wasn't as fast as Sarah but he managed to hold his own. He met the larger of the two gargoyles that charged him, shoving his body tight in against the creature's to avoid its claws as he pressed the barrel of his pistol to the underside of its skin and squeezed the trigger. The top of the creature's head erupted in a shower of blood that splashed over him as the bullet exited its skull. Walt slid away from the creature's dropping body only to be backhanded by the other creature. He heard and felt his jawbone break from the blow as it knocked him from his feet. The world was spinning before his eyes as he hit the street with a loud grunt. The gargoyle loomed over him, moving in for the kill, when suddenly its head blew apart as a high-velocity rifle round pulverized it.

Simon smiled at the success of his shot as he took aim at another of the gargoyles. The creatures were so focused on Walt and Sarah they seemed to have forgotten about him altogether. He shifted his rifle on the edge of the roof and fired again, dropping another gargoyle with a second headshot.

Sarah blocked the swiping claws of a gargoyle with the blade of her katana, severing the creature's fingers in the process. The gargoyle reeled back away from her. She whirled about like a ninja, full circle to shove the blade of her sword through its heart as she came around to face it again. The gargoyle looked down at its chest as Sarah yanked her blade free. Simon's rifle cracked a final time and the last of the gargoyles died, collapsing onto the street behind where she stood.

Walt was getting up as Sarah ran over to him.

"You okay?" she asked with concern in her eyes.

His fractured jaw kept him from answering her with words but he gave her a thumb's up.

Walt looked up and over at the rooftop Simon had been on only to see that sniper was gone. He was likely on his way down to meet up with them. The level was completed. All that was left to do was to get back inside the Beast and return to the Hub. Walt was ready for the pain he was in to go away. The transition to the Hub from this level would heal them like it always did and that couldn't happen soon enough for him.

"Where's Brent?" Sarah frowned.

Walt had lost sight of the big guy during the battle and had no idea. Unable to really answer her, he just shrugged.

Simon emerged from the building he had been on the roof of and came bounding across the street towards them. As he did, the Beast drove slowly up along the street to come to a stop near the trio. Cally flung its side door open and stepped out of the APC.

"Brent?" she asked, her voice trembling.

"Don't freak out," Simon cautioned her. "The big guy could very well be alive and wounded somewhere. It's just as good an explanation for why he hasn't respawned out here as what you are thinking. Whatever happened to Lee had to have been a fluke."

Cally had been utterly convinced that when Lee died on the previous level, he had died in the real world too. Walt didn't really think that was possible but he could understand why Cally was worried. There was no means for any of them to truly know what happened to Lee until they got back to the real world.

"Say, do you smell that?" Simon asked, sniffing at the air. "Kind of smells like somebody is having a cookout."

"I smell it too," Walt said. "Where's it coming from?"

Sarah frowned, looking at the diner. "I think I know but I really hope I'm wrong."

With Sarah in the lead, the team approached the front of the diner. Cally cried out and turned away as she saw Brent's smoldering combat armor and what was left of his body inside of it. Fat bubbled and popped and the big guy's skin had long been burnt away.

"Oh holy …" Simon started turning green. He dropped onto his knees and hands, vomiting onto the street before he could finish whatever he had been about to say.

Sarah crossed herself. Walt thought he heard her muttering a prayer for God to have mercy on Brent's soul. "His body isn't supposed to stay there like that," she said. "It's supposed to blink out when he dies so that it can be respawned."

Walt shrugged, not knowing what to say. He saw Cally whirl about and take off running. Walt went after her. Cally ran to the Beast, first leaning against its armored hull and then sliding down it to slump in the street. Her body shook with sobs as tears filled her eyes and overflowed to run along the curves of her cheeks. Walt removed his medkit from his pack and shot himself with a high-powered dose of painkiller.

"Cally," Walt mumbled as best he could through his broken jaw as he approached her to squat next to where she sat weeping.

"Don't, Walt," she warned him. "We all saw what happened to Lee. You guys didn't believe me, couldn't allow yourselves to really think that the game might have truly killed him. Now, Brent's gone too."

"You don't know that for sure, Cally," Walt reminded her, painfully forcing out each word as clearly as he could and hoping that Cally could understand what he was saying.

"Yes, I do. You and the others are in denial," Cally snapped at him, getting to her feet. "The truth about what's happening is too scary for you guys to deal with."

Sarah had walked over to join them.

"Brent's dead, Walt, we just saw his body. It's still there and it's not supposed to be. Why didn't he respawn? We're all supposed to respawn when we die. That's how the game works, right?" She pressed him for an answer as to what was going on.

"That's how it has always been before," Walt started, holding a hand against the side of his jaw. The talking he was forcing himself to do wasn't helping it in the slightest and the painkillers were wearing off fast. "I can't explain why it has changed, but apparently it has. Let's get back to the Hub and check out things more from there okay?"

"Okay," Sarah agreed. "But when we get back there, I'm out. I've had enough of this crap. The game is supposed to be fun not this sick … whatever the heck it is now."

The four of them loaded up in the Beast.

Level 3 complete! the voice of the game's AI bellowed as the Beast shimmered and blinked away, reappearing in the game's central Hub.

Sarah was first out of the APC as soon as it had finished transitioning into the Hub. Walt followed her out, thankful that his jaw had been healed and he was able to talk without near blinding pain coursing through his nerves.

Walt took a quick look around the Hub for Brent but just as Cally had told him, Brent wasn't there.

"Cally, go check on Brent in the real world. Simon, go with her," Walt ordered as he started after Sarah. She had headed straight for the logout station. He saw her cursing it and slamming a balled-up fist into its screen.

"What is it?" Walt asked carefully, hoping her anger wasn't about to be transferred to him.

"The blasted thing won't let me log out!" Sarah raged.

"That's impossible," Walt said, moving closer to the station to check it himself.

"You try it," Sarah spat at him.

Walt's fingers danced over the log station's keypad as he input the code to logout of the game. Instead of reappearing in the real world though, he was left standing there, staring at the flashing words "system error" on the station's screen.

"What the frag?" Walt mumbled in disbelief.

"You tell me," Sarah stared at him.

"This can't be," Walt stammered. "The game *has* to let you out when you're ready."

"Apparently not anymore," Sarah snarled.

Cally and Simon came up behind them.

"Brent's dead too," Cally whimpered through trembling lips.

"We don't know that!" Simon snapped. "For all we know, he's just unconscious out there!"

Cally spun to punch Simon in the stomach. Caught utterly by surprise, Simon grunted and doubled over as her small fist buried itself in his guts.

"You're an idiot!" Cally wailed at the sniper.

Walt grabbed her by the arms before she started hitting Simon again. She struggled against his hold as Simon got his wind back and rose up to glare at her with blazing anger in his eyes.

"Don't even think about it," Sarah warned, stepping between Simon and Cally.

Simon flung up his hands in a gesture of peace and backed slowly away from Sarah.

"Hey," he said, "she's the one who hit me."

"You had it coming, you bastard!" Cally shrieked.

"Cally!" Walt snapped at her. "Get yourself together! Now!"

Walt waited until she had at least seemed to calm down before he released his grip on her arms. When he did, she jerked away from him.

"None of you want to hear it much less accept it, but I am telling you that Lee and Brent are dead! D – E – A – D, dead!" Cally cried.

"And we're stuck in here," Sarah added.

"What did you just say?" Simon asked, his eyes going wide.

"I said we're stuck in here, Simon. Walt and I both tried to logout of the game. It wouldn't let us. The station just kept flashing the words system error over and over," Sarah told him.

Simon shoved Sarah and Cally out of his way moving to the station to try to logout himself. He input his exit code but nothing happened. The words "system error" flashed on the screen as he stared at it, his mind not wanting to believe they were real.

"That's impossible," Simon said nearly on the edge of tears.

"I said the exact same thing but clearly it's not," Walt told the sniper.

"Someone or something has trapped us in this game," Cally spoke up.

"So you don't think it's just a glitch in the game or a series of malfunctions in its operating system?" Walt asked.

Cally shook her head. "Too many things all happening at the same time for it just to be the game messing up, someone has to be doing this with intent."

"Why?" Sarah demanded. "Who would want to frag about with us?"

"Better question," Walt said, "who would want us dead? We're just a bunch of ordinary gamers. I mean, none of us are anything special in the real world, right?"

"I am a computer engineering student," Cally said. "I can't imagine that would tick anyone off."

"I drive a cab," Sarah commented.

"I live with my mom in her apartment," Simon admitted. "I don't have a job at the moment. I'm looking though."

Walt grunted as the last part of what Simon said had the edge of a lie to it.

"What about you, Walt?" Sarah asked.

"I'm a teacher at a small college in North Carolina," Walt told her.

"Yay! So we're all really boring, maybe even pathetic in own ways," Sarah said. "That's fantastic and all, but it doesn't tell us squat about why this is happening to us."

"What we need to do is find a way to get out of the game." Walt looked at Cally. "Is there any other means of doing so besides officially logging out?"

Cally nodded. "One way ..."

"Oh don't tell me …" Sarah started.

"Yep," Cally confirmed her fear. "The only other way out of the game is to beat it."

Simon was on the verge of losing it entirely. "Whoa, hold up, little girl. Are you saying you want us to go back out there and take on another level knowing full well that if we die, we're dead?"

"Just a few minutes ago, Simon, you were arguing that Brent and Lee weren't dead, remember?" Cally shot him a bitter grin. "I guess you're really listening to me now, aren't you?"

"We could stay here in the Hub," Sarah pointed out. "Wait for someone out there in the real world to realize something is up with us. Surely someone will have to eventually and then they'll get us all out."

"Normally, I would agree with that," Cally said, "but I don't think whoever or whatever is behind all this is going to let that happen. The game itself should have alerted people out there to Lee and Brent's conditions but it hasn't so far as we can tell. They appear to be alone and left exactly where they died."

"That brings up a good point." Walt smiled, feeling proud of himself for thinking of it. "How do we even know those images of Lee and Brent that we've seen are real? They could just as easily be fakes created by whoever is doing this to us."

"You're right, Walt. They very well could be but the question is – are we prepared to take that gamble?" Cally asked him. "If they are real and we die in here, then we end up exactly like them."

"Could all this just be some sort of prank?" Sarah jumped in. "Maybe some hacker just messing around with us for fun?"

"There's no way to know anything for sure except that everything we have seen points to our two friends being dead for real out there and we do know that we are trapped in here," Cally reminded them all. "If we want out of this game, we're going to have to finish it and that's that unless whoever or whatever is holding us in here just suddenly decides to let us go. And I don't see that happening."

"Frag me," Simon muttered. "I don't want to die."

"None of us do, Simon," Cally snapped at the sniper. "But the fact is we need to gear up and get on with the next level and the sooner the better."

"You're really serious about going back out there, aren't you?" Sarah sounded stunned by Cally's apparent bravery.

"The game penalizes anyone who stays in the Hub for too long," Cally told them. "It's an odd rule and one that a lot folks don't even know about but it happens. We're pushing the limits of how long we're allowed to stay to gear up and pick our next level path as it is. I, for one, don't want to know what kind of penalty gets dealt out by a game that's already killing folks, do you?"

"God have mercy on us." Walt ran his fingers through the front of his hair. It was a nervous habit for him and one that he had always claimed helped him to find his center and think.

"Okay," Walt said, taking charge of the situation. "Let's pick our next level and get moving before whatever time limit we have in here runs out. Cally?"

"For the next level, we've got a choice of blowing up a building infected by a demon virus or taking on good old-fashioned sewer monsters," Cally said.

"The demon thing sounds a lot like the zombie level we started with," Sarah commented.

"It's very close to it," Cally agreed. "Just a higher difficulty level, of course."

"And the sewer monsters?" Walt asked.

"It's a hunting level like the werewolf one was supposed to be," Cally said. "Think of it like an old-school dungeon crawl."

"I vote for the demon virus," Sarah said. "It's an easier goal. We get in, plant a bomb, and run like hell before we blow the place."

Cally nodded. "I agree. The sewers we'd a lot more likely to be forced to split up and there is always the chance the monsters down there would come at us like the werewolves did. Their individual power levels are a lot higher than the infected demon ones."

"Simon?" Walt asked, looking at the openly trembling sniper.

"I don't want any part of either one," Simon replied, shaking his head.

"You don't have a choice, Simon," Cally said. "If you stay here beyond the allowed time limit, who knows what will happen to you? You could just fall over dead for all we know."

"The deciding vote is yours then, Walt," Sarah said, turning to him.

"Demons," Walt answered. "Everybody gear up and get to the Beast A.S.A.P."

****

Five minutes later, the team was in the Beast. Simon sat in the rear, his sniper rifle propped against his seat next to him, hugging himself and rocking back and forth. It had taken everything Walt had just to get the man into the APC. Walt didn't like Simon being part of the team for the mission that lay ahead of them but leaving him in the Hub alone wasn't an option. If Walt left him and Simon died there, he knew that he would never forgive himself. Still, bringing him along in such a state was just as dangerous to everyone else. They didn't have time to babysit Simon. They needed to get into the building where the demon virus was loose and blow it as quickly as they could.

Sarah looked up from where she sat across from Simon, holding her katana in her lap. She had been running the tip of one of her fingers over its blade before Walt had drawn her attention. Walt could tell from her expression that she had to be thinking the same things he was about Simon. For the moment, there was nothing either of them could do but worry though and hope that Simon snapped out of it once the action got rolling.

Cally was in the driver's seat, running system checks on the Beast when Walt walked into the forward compartment to take the seat next to her.

"All systems green," she told him. "We're good to go."

Walt nodded, doing his best to give her a reassuring smile. "Take us out then."

The Beast rolled forward and disappeared from the Hub. It reappeared, driving along what was in every way a normal city street in the midst of late-night traffic. Up ahead, Walt could see the flashing of blue lights surrounding a building and he knew that was where they were headed for.

"This level requires that we interact with some NPCs on the way into the building," Cally informed him. "Shouldn't be a big deal as long as we don't let them slow us down too much."

"Right," Walt said. "Looks like the cops and some special unit folks have that building sealed off tight. Take us in as close as you can though."

Cally drove the Beast straight up the barricades surrounding the building and killed its engine next to them. Two heavily armed S.W.A.T officers approached the APC as the team opened its side door and emerged from it.

"Officers." Walt smiled at them, giving the two men a nod of respect as he flashed his Monster Shooter ID at them.

The officers relaxed some at the sight of it.

Another officer who was clearly a lieutenant came up from behind them. "I can't tell you how happy we are that you guys are finally here," he said, extending his hand to Walt.

Walt accepted it and shook it firmly. Switching on the enhanced perception of the game world that being a player character sometimes allowed him, Walt appraised the LT and the other two cops. The LT registered as a Level 2 NPC, the others Level 1. Neither was out of the ordinary. It made sense that an NPC with the rank of lieutenant would be a Level 2. Odds were his bit of programming had been around long enough for him to get the level/rank bump. Turning his eyes to the crowd of gawkers surrounding the barricade, Walt looked them over too. Just as he suspected, they were all Level 0 civilians.

"Sir?" the LT asked and Walt realized he hadn't spoken to the man yet.

"Sorry, Lieutenant, my mind was elsewhere," Walt replied, sighing. "These three with me are my team. We'll get into the building A.S.A.P. and get this outbreak dealt with."

"Glad to hear it, sir," the LT said. "The sooner, the better. Things are getting a bit edgy out here with the civvies. The ones with family trapped on the inside are beginning to cause some serious problems."

"You just hold on and keep them in line," Walt told the LT. "We'll handle the virus."

"Have you picked an entry point yet?" the lieutenant asked.

Walt chuckled and shook his head. "We just got here, Lieutenant."

"Oh yeah. Right. Sorry about that." The lieutenant looked embarrassed, his cheeks flushing red.

"I think the front door is as good as any." Sarah pointed at the steps leading up to it as she moved to stand beside Walt.

The lieutenant ogled her for a moment and then appeared to realize he was doing so and quickly started staring at the steps she had pointed at.

Sarah wasn't a supermodel or anything, but not even Walt could deny that there was something appealing about her. It was more than just her tone body or slightly above average good looks. It was how she carried herself or something. Even now with her confidence shaken by the unexplainable mess the team was in, she came across as tougher than he did, Walt admitted to himself.

"The front door, huh?" the lieutenant asked, keeping his eyes trained on it. "That's a pretty straightforward approach. I figured you guys would go in through the roof or a window or something."

"Don't let the movies fool you, son," Walt said, playing the part of his character in the game. "Sometimes the most direct way is the best way."

"Right," the lieutenant said, though he sounded like he didn't believe a word of what Walt had just told him. "I'll let my men know."

"Do that," Walt ordered him. "We don't need to be shot in the back on the way up those steps."

The lieutenant scowled at Walt in response to the jab at his men's competence but otherwise let it slide then hurried off to pass along the word that the team was going in, barking orders through the radio he carried as he went.

"Good kid that one," Sarah commented. "Not bad on the eyes on either."

Walt laughed. "Come on. The longer we wait, the more demons there's bound to be waiting for us."

****

The crowd of civilians cheered and shouted out as the team of four monster shooters headed up the steps to the building's main entrance. The cops and S.W.A.T. officers watched the team carefully as they went too, keeping an eye out for any trouble the monster shooters might bring with them that would allow the demons to get out of the building as they entered it. Walt ignored all of it. He had traded his normal AK-47 for a pair of pump-action shotguns. He carried one in his hands, shell ready in its chamber, and the other strapped to his back. Walt didn't really know why he had switched out weapons at the last minute. Maybe it was to honor Brent somehow as the big guy had always had a thing for shotguns. Or maybe it was just because he figured as up close to the demons as they were bound to be in the corridors of the building, the stopping power and spread of a shotgun blast would be good things to have.

The front doors of the building were made of transparent security glass. There was no sign of any demons lurking in the shadows of the lobby directly behind them. That made sense. The demons would focus on infecting everyone in the building with their pestilence and growing their numbers as much as they could before they made any attempt to break through the police lines outside. Walt didn't really know if he believed that "virus demons" were truly intelligent like a human was, but the creatures were as bugger-all cunning as any monsters he had ever faced. Their survival instincts were honed to a razor edge based on his previous encounters with their like.

Shooting their way in through the front doors wasn't an option. The doors needed to stay intact to help contain the demons in the building. Walt gestured at Cally.

"It looks to be clear in there," Walt told her. "Can you get these doors open and then relocked?"

"I'm on it," Cally said, letting the P-90 she carried swing from her shoulder by its strap as she dug into the contents of the toolkit on her belt and started work on the doors. The job took her less than two minutes. The doors swung inward as Cally stood up, tucking away her tools.

"After you, boss," she said, grinning at Walt.

Simon was hanging back and looking like he didn't want to go into the building at all. Walt knew he was going to have to stick close to the sniper if only to keep him from getting the rest of the team into serious trouble.

"Sarah, you mind taking point on this one?" Walt looked over at her.

"Thought you would never ask," she answered, shooting him a feral grin.

With her katana strapped to her back and her twin pistols drawn and in her hands, Sarah led the team into the building. Once they were all inside, Cally paused long enough to make sure the doors were closed and resealed behind them.

The power appeared to be on in most of the building from the outside but it wasn't inside the lobby area. The only illumination came from the flashing blues and reds of the police cars and the street lights from out in the street beyond the doors they had just entered. It was enough to see by in terms of moving around, but it left entire areas of the lobby covered in shadows.

"Are we taking the elevator or the stairs?" Sarah asked, glancing over her shoulder at Walt.

"Stairs," Cally answered before Walt could respond. "The power seems to be 'iffy' in this building and the last thing any of us want is to get stuck in an elevator shaft, hanging there waiting on the demons to come to us. At least with the stairs, however narrow they might be, we'll have *some* room to maneuver."

"Stairs it is then," Walt agreed.

Sarah cautiously approached the door to the stairwell leading up from the lobby to the building's other floors. She holstered one of her pistols to reach out and try its knob. The door was unlocked.

"On three," she told the others. "One … Two … Three!"

Sarah flung the door inward and dove through it, redrawing the pistol she holstered as she moved. Nothing sprang from the stairwell at her as she entered it and the lights were on.

"Clear!" she called to the rest of the team as she neared the bottom of the stairs and waited on the others to catch up to her before starting up them.

Simon was sweating like a pig. His skin was drenched and his hair slicked to his head beneath his helmet. He looked sickly pale as he continued to bring up the team's rear.

"How far are we going up?" Walt asked Cally.

"In order to place the bomb in my pack at the optimum spot and ensure this whole building goes, we need to reach the fifth floor," she answered.

"Really?" Walt said. "I figured we'd have to go up a lot higher."

"Not this time," Cally replied, laughing. "The way this place is built, taking out the fifth floor will bring it all crashing down."

Sarah froze on the steps above them. She had just rounded the turn in the stairs that led onto the platform outside the doorway into the fourth floor. Her hand shot up, signaling for them to stop as well.

"We've got company coming," Sarah whispered. "Listen."

Walt heard the movement in the stairwell above them, quiet but quick steps pounding down the stairwell towards their position. It was impossible to tell how many of the demons there were from the noise but it was clearly more than just a couple of the creatures.

"Looks like we might have to go *through* them, Walt," Sarah told him. "They'll be hitting the fifth-floor platform at the same time we do if we keep moving."

"Nothing for it then," Walt said, shrugging. "Everybody get ready. Things may get pretty rough."

"I can't do this, Walt," Simon whimpered.

"You got no choice, buddy," Walt said to the sniper. "Man up, or let those things tear you apart. It's up to you."

Walt turned back to Sarah and gave her the signal to start moving again. She led the way up onto the fifth-floor platform as the first of the demons appeared out the shadows, bounding down the steps above it. The demon's eyes glowed a sickly yellow in the darkness as it lunged at Sarah. Sarah's twin pistols came up blazing. Her first shot blew a chunk of flesh from the creature's shoulder. Her second took out a piece of its throat, spraying sickish, green blood onto the stairwell wall as it toppled forward. Its death did nothing to slow the other demons behind it. Their snarls and hisses echoed in the narrow space of the stairwell. Sarah turned to try the doorway leading onto the fifth floor as Walt and Cally moved up to cover her. Walt's shotgun boomed as he fired into the monsters. Two of the demons crumped from the blast as Cally opened up with her P-90 hosing those behind them. Simon continued to hold back though he had managed to force himself to move up onto the platform with the rest of the team.

"The door's locked!" Sarah shouted, moving to trade places with Cally so that the tech could work her magic on it. Simon got in her way though as she whirled about almost tripping her up.

"Snap out of it, you fragging coward!" Sarah shoved Simon from her path.

Walt's shotgun thundered three more times in rapid succession. "A little help here!" he shouted. The demons were gaining ground towards the platform with each passing second, despite his attempts to hold them at bay. Walt fired again. His shot punched a hole through the lead demon as its guts were blown out its back.

"I'm out!" Walt screamed, moving back to reload as Sarah moved up to take his place. It was too little too late though even with as fast as her pistols barked. She sent three more of the monsters back to hell before they overran her. One grabbed a fistful of her hair, trying to pull her forward as another leaped onto her legs. Most of the hair the demon clutched was torn free of Sarah's scalp as she wailed in pain and was tugged to the stairwell floor by the other demon trying to take a bite out of her thighs. Sarah ignored the pain she was in and focused on keeping herself from being infected by the second demon. She lashed out with the butt of her right pistol, bashing in its nose; bone crunched as the pistol's butt met it. Sarah caught hold of the demon's throat while its head was reared back with her left hand and held it tight as she brought the barrel of her right pistol up under the monster's chin and squeezed its trigger. The demon's brains left its head through the top of its skull. Sarah let go of the thing's corpse, scooping up her dropped left pistol as she rolled away from it. Another demon came flopping down towards her, trying to land on top of her where she lay. Both her pistols fired in unison, turning its eyes into pulp inside their sockets. The dead demon thudded into the platform next to her as she scrambled back to her feet.

Something must have snapped inside of Simon because as Sarah saw that there were now demons both behind and in front of her where some of the monsters had gotten past her, the sniper screamed at the top of his lungs as he sprang forward to her aid. Simon plowed into the three demons that had slipped by her. Using his rifle like a staff held out in front of him, he knocked two of the monsters off the stairs' railing. Their cries rang out as they fell towards the ground floor below. The third demon had only been clipped by the butt of Simon's rifle and had avoided being pushed over the railing. Its claws flashed through the air as it moved to take a swipe at Simon's face. Sarah put a bullet into its knuckles, causing the monster to jerk its hand back in the fraction of a second before her second shot dug into the center of its forehead. Both she and Simon were in a poor position to defend themselves as the demons continued to bound down the stairs onto the platform. Thankfully, Walt had reloaded and stepped between them and the incoming demons.

"Run!" Walt shouted at them. "Cally has the door open!"

Neither of them needed to be told twice. They sprinted for the door as Walt fired into the mass of demons, pumped a fresh shell into the chamber of his shotgun, and fired again as began to make a fighting retreat himself.

Cally added the fire of her P-90 to help cover Walt as he backed up to the doorway. Both of them ducked onto the fifth floor as Sarah slammed the door shut in their wake. Cally struggled to get the door locked back into place as quickly as she could as Sarah and Simon kept their full strength and weight braced against it, holding back the demons on its other side. The lock snapped into place with a loud click.

"That's not going to hold them for long!" Cally warned, already turning to sprint down the corridor away from the doorway.

"She's right," Walt said. "Let's move!"

The door shook in its frame as Sarah and Simon released it to race after Cally. Walt waited until they were past him, taking it upon himself to act as the team's rearguard. He was glad to see that Simon had at least somewhat gotten it together again, but he wasn't ready to trust him fully again yet.

Walt heard the door burst inward behind him, ripped from its hinges as he rounded the bend of the corridor that the others had taken.

"In here!" Cally was waving to him from a side door in the corridor.

He made it inside and they got the door shut before the demons ever made it into sight. Walt and Cally held their breath as they heard the demons go tearing along the corridor outside past the room they were in.

Walt smiled at Cally. "Good thinking, kiddo."

"Don't you ever call me that again, boss," she said, grinning.

"Yes, ma'am." Walt took a look about the room they had ducked into. It looked to be some kind of conference room. It was wide and spacious with a massive, long table surrounded by chairs taking up the bulk of its center. There were blood stains on the room's carpet but no bodies or demons around for the team to worry about.

"So what do we do now?" Sarah asked.

"We get back out there and get Cally's bomb to where it needs to go," Walt said.

"That mess in the stairwell with the locked door; that was as bad as anything we likely would've faced if we had gone after the sewer monsters would've been. I'm not for a repeat of it anytime soon," Sarah said. "If Cally's going to need time to get the bomb set, we're going to need a diversion, something to draw the demons away from wherever she'll be working. We might not get as lucky as we did in the stairwell if we let those things hem us in like that again."

"Did you have something in mind?" Walt asked.

"Actually, I do," Sarah answered. "Cally, the spot where you need to set up the bomb is at the end of this corridor, right?"

Cally nodded. "Yep. There's a load-bearing section there that needs to go. We collapse it and this whole place will come down."

"Let Simon cover her, Walt, while the two of us head on up to the sixth floor and kick a little demon arse," Sarah suggested. "We should be able to make more than enough of a ruckus to have every demon anywhere near us to be drawn to it."

"That's pretty damn risky given how things are with the game," Walt pointed out.

"I didn't say it was a perfect plan," Sarah replied, shrugging.

"I don't like leaving Cally alone with Simon," Walt said.

"Hey!" Cally and Simon both shot him glares.

"I'm right here, man." Simon frowned at him. "I can hear you."

"And I can take care of myself," Cally said. "If Simon goes all cowardly crybaby again, I can just let the demons have him while I get the heck out."

Walt and Sarah laughed.

"Bugger it all," Simon roared. "This ain't easy for any of us now. Stop pretending it is."

"If we give into our fears, none of us will ever make it out of this game alive," Sarah said. "We aren't going to beat even this level if we just try to play it safe all the time."

"Okay," Walt jumped in, taking over the conversation. "We've got a plan. Sarah and I are going to head out if the coast is clear. You'll know it's time to get moving when you hear the gunfire on the next floor up. Got it?"

Cally and Simon nodded.

"You take care of her, man," Walt reminded Simon a final time, whispering the words to the sniper as he moved to the room's door. Sarah was already there with her ear pressed against it, listening for any sign of the demons in the corridor outside.

"Seems clear," she told him. "You ready?"

"Just open the blasted door," Walt urged her.

Sarah cautiously opened the door and the two of them crept out into the corridor as Simon closed it after them. The area was clear of demons.

"How do you want to do this?" Sarah whispered.

"You take the left, I'll take the right. We'll meet up on the next floor. If I hear you open up, I'll do the same and vice versa. That way we'll be as sure as we can be to draw the demons away from Cally and Simon down here," Walt said.

"Roger that," Sarah replied.

****

Lights flickered along the ceiling of the corridor as Sarah made her way to the stairwell leading up to the next floor. There was one on each side of the floor and Walt would be taking the other one up. The stairwell door was unlocked. She paused to sneak a glance through its small slot of a window and saw that it looked to be clear. As quietly as she could, she opened the doorway and entered the stairwell. Her matching pistols were holstered on her hips. Sarah knew she would need them later, but for now, stealth was her priority. She drew her katana as she started up the steps to the next floor. Getting into melee-range combat with monsters that could infect you with the virus they carried in their blood from a single scratch of their claws wasn't ideal. These demons weren't like zombies. They moved with speed and strength that was enhanced by the virus they carried.

Sarah had feared there would still be a large number of demons still inside the stairwell given how the team had been driven out of it not long ago, but there wasn't. It was clear. The demons had moved on somewhere else in search of prey. As she rounded the corner of the stairs leading up to the door to the next floor, Sarah spotted a single demon up the stairs from her. It saw her at the same time. Its yellow eyes blazed brighter at the sight of her as it gave a roar and sprang forward to meet her.

The claws of the demon's right hand lashed out, swiping towards her. Sarah dodged the attack and countered with one of her own. Her katana flickered through the air, its blade sinking into the flesh of the demon's arm. Bone crunched and gave way to the metal as the demon's arm was severed from its body close to the elbow. The arm flopped wetly onto the stairs as the demon reeled away from her. Sarah pressed her attack, closing in for the kill. The blade of her katana lashed out again, catching the demon across its throat and opening it up. The creature's foul blood splattered over her as she took another step closer and kicked the flailing demon in its chest. The kick sent it teetering over the railing of the stairs to vanish into the darkness beyond it. She heard its body crash into the ground floor below. Her victory was a hollow one though as she heard the voices of several more demons in the stairwell apparently below her position raise their voices, howling and screeching inhuman cries. Their footfalls pounded up the stairs towards where she stood. She could tell that there couldn't be more than a handful of the monsters and made the choice to take them on here and now before entering the floor she had been heading to.

The first of the demons came bounding up at her. Both of its hands were outstretched before it, grasping at her as it came. Sarah's blade entered the demon's guts in the middle of its stomach. She jerked it upwards, opening up the monster from the sword's point of entry to edge of its sternum. The demon twitched on her blade, trying to tear free of it as spittle flew from its lips and it thrashed about in pain. Sarah jerked her blade free of the demon's body. It flopped onto the stairs to her left, making a grab for her ankles despite the amount of damage she had inflicted on it. She had no time to finish it though as two more demons lunged at her.

Sarah hopped backwards, up a couple of steps, as she struggled to keep the two demons off of her. She still wasn't ready to switch over to her pistols. Her blade split open the nose of one of the demons and then slashed into the second's snarling mouth on its back swing. The blade of her katana removed several of the demon's teeth and part of its open, lower jaw. The demon stumbled, tumbling back down over the steps it had raced up to get at her as the other demon shook off the pain from its mangled nose and came at her again. Its claws sparked against the plating of the combat armor covering her shoulder. The blow staggered her but Sarah stayed on her feet, recovering quickly, to punch the demon in its forehead. Its head snapped back as she followed up by bringing her katana around in a wide arc so that its blade slashed along the length of the demon's chest. Blood flew from the wound but the demon continued to come at her relentlessly. Sarah did her best to get out of the monster's way but it managed to grab her. She felt its superhumanly strong fingers latch onto her shoulders as its face jutted forward, teeth snapping at her neck. Sarah was forced to let go of her katana as she used the creature's own strength and momentum against it, slinging it on past her into the stairs. Its face smashed into the steps behind the ones she had been standing on. Bone caved inward as the sole of her right boot came down on the backside of the creature's head before it could get up to drive its skull hard into the steps. She knew she had successfully fragged up the creature's skull, fracturing it from how the monster's body lay there twitching on the steps in front of her.

She didn't see or hear the demon coming at her from behind until it was too late. The monster's arms wrapped around her arms, pinning them to her sides as it lifted her from the steps. Sarah reared her head back in a desperate move, driving it into the demon's face just above its snarling lips. The impact stunned the thing enough for her to worm free of its hold on her. As she landed on the steps with a grunt of pain, Sarah rolled over to face the demon and kicked out with both of her legs. Her feet caught the demon in the chest as it threw itself at her. The move flung the demon backwards into the wall of the stairwell. Sarah raced to reclaim her katana as the demon recovered and came at her again.

The blade of her katana entered the underside of the monster's chin. Its tip emerged through the top of the demon's skull, sealing its mouth shut and destroying its brain. Sarah let go of the sword and ran for the door leading onto the floor she had been headed for before she had been attacked. She slung it open and sprinted along the corridor behind it. Her pistols cleared their holsters as she drew them with blinding speed.

Sarah kept her flat-out pace as she raced along the corridor. A demon popped out of a room ahead of her and she put a bullet into its brain. The monster died instantly, collapsing to fall into her path. She leaped over it as she continued on. Others demons were coming out of the woodwork now. They came from side rooms, dropped from where they clung to the corridor's ceiling, and poured along the corridor from its other end on a direct path for her. Sarah skidded to a halt, knowing that it was time to stand and fight. The only things she had to do now were stay alive and make as much noise as possible.

****

Walt's path had taken him parallel to Sarah's up the stairwell on the other side of the floor where Cally and Simon would prep the bomb to blow the building. He hadn't encountered any resistance in the stairwell and was thankful for it. He wasn't the "close in" fighter that Sarah was with her sword. *His own methods were louder*, he thought with a wry smile as he double-checked the pump-action shotgun he carried to make sure it was ready. He carried a second shotgun slung onto his back by its strap and a pistol holstered on his hip. His plan was to get to where he needed to go and just start lighting things up so to speak.

Stepping into the corridor outside of the stairwell, he heard gunfire erupt in the distance and knew it belonged to Sarah. She had to have made it onto the floor and was already busy drawing the attention of the demons in the building to her. Walt hurried along the corridor at a careful but hurried pace trying to reach her. That wasn't supposed to be the plan. He was supposed to just start killing demons as soon as he encountered one and hopefully give the monsters a second target to go after. Walt had to force himself to stop and get a grip on that fact. Knowing that any of them could actually die in the game now, it was a hard thing to do.

A cluster of demons burst from a doorway ahead of him. They didn't see him. Their attention was focused in the direction of the gunfire and they took off towards it. Or rather they would have had he not given them a little surprise. Walt raised the barrel of his shotgun at the demons and fired. The blast slammed into the monsters from behind, cutting them down. Two of the demons died instantly while the third staggered to lean against the wall of the corridor with strands of its guts hanging out of its ruptured side. Walt pumped another round into the chamber of his shotgun as he sprinted towards the surviving demon. He didn't have any intention of using the round on the badly wounded monster, but it was better to have the weapon ready for when more of the monsters showed themselves than not.

The wounded demon spun to face him as he ran at it. Its yellow eyes went wide as Walt reached it and rammed the butt of his shotgun into its face with the force of his full strength and the momentum he'd built up combined. Bone shattered as the demon's nose folded inward and its cheekbones crumpled. The demon was knocked into the wall by the blow and bounced off of it to topple to the corridor's floor. Walt brought the butt of his shotgun down onto the backside of its skull to make sure the demon wasn't getting up again.

The sound of the shotgun's blast had done its job in getting the attention of the other demons on this side of the floor as Walt looked up to see close to a dozen of the monsters spilling into the corridor from various rooms. Snarling and howling, they raced at him.

Walt slipped a grenade from the pouch on his belt that rested opposite his holstered pistol, pulled its pin with a quick motion of his thumb, and lobbed it at the approaching demons. He dove through the open doorway of a nearby room as the grenade landed among the ranks of the demons and exploded. The explosion seemed to shake the floor beneath him and the very walls of the room he had ducked into. As soon as it was over though, Walt flung himself back out into the corridor. Several patches of the corridor's wall were on fire and mangled body parts of the demons were scattered everywhere.

A few of the monsters were still alive, though badly hurt, and trying to rise to their feet. Walt drew his pistol, walking among them as he dispatched them all one by one with well-placed shots to their heads. Finishing them off in such a fashion was gruesome work but it had to be done. He couldn't take the chance of any of them getting up and following after him from behind nor did he want to waste his shotgun's ammo on such work when he didn't need to.

He could still hear the cracks of Sarah's pistols in the distance as he sent the last of the grenade-torn demons back to Hell. Walt just hoped Sarah could hold on until he made it to her. As tough and deadly as she was, she was still just one person and Walt had no intention of letting her keep fighting the monsters alone.

Walt darted through the corridors of the floor, making his way towards the sound of gunfire. He came flying around a corner and found himself face to face with a demon. It snarled as its claws lashed out at him. Walt threw himself sideways, his shoulder slamming into the wall of the corridor, narrowly avoiding the creature's attack. Cursing himself for being so careless, he thrust the barrel of his shotgun into the demon's throat as if it were a spear. The demon staggered away from him, clutching its injured throat and gasping for air. Walt followed up, swinging the butt of his shotgun around in a wide arc. It smashed into the side of the demon's skull with the rewarding sound of cracking bone. Walt left the demon where it lay, running on by it.

"About time you got here!" he heard Sarah yell at him as he came bursting into the corridor where she was making her stand. Bodies of demons littered the floor around her as she was hurriedly reloading one of her revolvers.

"Move!" Walt shouted at her as he jerked up his shotgun and leveled it at a demon coming at her from behind.

Sarah threw herself flat as Walt's shotgun thundered. The blast lifted the demon from the floor and sent it sprawling backwards, its chest a ragged mass of spraying blood and shredded tissue. Sarah was back on her feet by the time its corpse hit the floor. She snapped the loaded chamber of her revolver shut and flashed Walt a wild grin. The grin became a frown as both of them realized that the corridor was empty other than the two of them.

"What the frag?" Sarah muttered. "Those things were coming like crazy until you showed up. Why did they stop?"

"Maybe I scared them off," Walt joked, trying to cut the tension as they both looked around in disbelief that they were alone.

"I doubt it," Sarah huffed. "If they've all suddenly gone after Cally and Simon, we're dead."

"We'd hear gunfire below us if they had," Walt tried to reassure her. "The two of them wouldn't go down without a fight."

"I hope you're right," Sarah said.

The sound of splintering wood drew their attention to the far end of the corridor behind Sarah. The wall there exploded into the corridor as something massive plunged through and crashed into the wall across from it. As the demon that had come through the wall rose to its full height, Walt stared at it. The thing looked like a cross between a cartoon and a nightmare. The infected man had surely been a bodybuilder or something before he had become infected. When the demon virus entered his blood and amped his strength and reflexes, his muscles had grown to what would have been comical proportions if he wasn't trying to kill them. The eight foot tall, muscle-bound demon roared its fury as it charged at the two of them and Sarah stepped behind him. Walt pumped a round into the chamber of his shot and fired. The blast caught the demon dead on but didn't even slow it down.

"Walt!" Sarah shouted as she saw he wasn't going to be able to escape the demon's path in time. She didn't have a clear shot at the monster with Walt between her and it.

The demon plowed into Walt. The impact lifted him off his feet and hurled him down the corridor. Sarah dodged Walt's flailing form as it flew by her. She had no idea how badly hurt he was and no time to check on him. Sarah found herself facing the giant demon as it came charging towards her. Only one of her revolvers was loaded. The other was holstered on her belt. She popped off three shots at the giant demon. Two smacked into its shoulder, digging into the monster's flesh. Her third shot struck its forehead but not getting any penetration through the demon's thick bone there.

Sarah ducked as the giant demon took a swipe at her. The monster's fist swooshed over her, taking out a section of the corridor wall in an explosion of shattering plaster and splintering wood. Several of the splinters pierced the exposed skin of the back of her neck. Sarah flinched at the pain as the demon pressed its attack. Joining its two hands together into one massive downward swing, it struck at her again. Sarah jumped to the side. The demon's blow broke through the corridor's floor, leaving a ring of jagged wood where they hit it.

Landing on her feet to the demon's right, Sarah fired again. Her revolver spat lead at the monster as its barrel flashed. The first bullet punched the side of the demon's skull, doing nothing more than further angering it. The second took off the tip of its ear. The demon howled, rising up to its full height at the pain. Its head smashed through the corridor's ceiling. It took the demon a moment to free itself and Sarah used the time to run like hell. She sprinted to where Walt was regaining consciousness and beginning to sit up.

"Come on!" she yelled at Walt, jerking him to his feet. "We have to move!"

Walt grunted, clearly disoriented, but followed her lead. They raced along the corridor together with the demon on their heels. It roared after them. Sarah glanced over her shoulders into its blazing, angry eyes. A chill shuddered through her. The already-hulking demon honestly seemed to be growing as it continued after them as if its hate and rage were feeding it, increasing its power.

As if coming out of a trance, Walt began to get himself together as they ran. He had lost his shotgun and unslung the spare one he carried on his back, pumping a round into its chamber. The end of the corridor was coming up ahead of them quickly. He thanked God that the doorway leading into the stairwell was open. He followed Sarah through it. The giant demon chasing them smashed into and through the doorway like a runaway eighteen-wheeler. Chunks of the wall around the doorway flew over the stairs as the demon burst into the stairwell behind them. The stairs themselves shook from its weight as it roared and charged after them again.

They were leading the thing straight to Cally and Simon. Walt knew they couldn't let that happen. They were going to have to turn and face the thing, stop it somehow. For all its size and strength, the thing could still be hurt. Walt whirled about, aiming the barrel of his shotgun up at the giant demon as it bounded down the stairs. Taking aim at its knees, he squeezed the shotgun's trigger. The shotgun bucked in his hands as it thundered in the tight space of the stairwell. The demon had been mauling the stairs' railing as it came, too wild and wide to be hemmed in by it. Walt's shot tore into its knees, blowing the meat there from the bones. The giant demon howled in pain and fury losing its already limited footing on the stairs. It careened over the side of the stairs and fell from them. Walt heard the giant demon crash into the bottom of the stairwell several floors below.

"That isn't going to stop it," Sarah said, coming to a halt in front of him near the doorway leading onto the floor where Cally and Simon were supposed to be setting up the bomb to blow the building.

"I know," Walt said sadly. "Listen … It's already on its way back up."

The sound of the giant demon's heavy and hurried footfalls rang out in the stairwell. Walt could hear the thing snarling as it came.

"We've got to find a way to stop it," Sarah told him.

"I'm hoping you have something in mind because I got nothing," Walt replied.

Sarah shook her head.

"Go get Simon!" he ordered her. "Maybe the three of us together can put enough rounds into this monster to make it stay down. I'll hold it here until you get back."

Sarah stared at him. "You'll hold it here?"

"Just go!" Walt snapped at her as he pumped a fresh round into the chamber of his shotgun and positioned himself to get a clear line of fire at where the monster would be coming up the stairs. He glanced over to see that Sarah was done arguing with him. She had slung open the doorway to the floor they were outside of and vanished through it. Walt gave a grunt of satisfaction at her departure and then settled in to face the giant demon alone.

Though there was light in the stairwell, it was still the eyes of the giant demon that he saw come into view first. They glowed like tiny fireballs of pure, supernatural hate. Walt didn't hesitate. He took the shot he had been waiting for at the monster. The blast from his shotgun peppered its face, shoulders, and upper body with holes. The giant demon roared but didn't fall. Instead, it increased its speed up the stairs, mangling the railing to its right as it climbed them. Walt fired again, aiming for thing's forehead. The blast hammered the creature but still didn't even so much as slow it.

Walt knew he was dead if the giant demon got within reach of him. He whirled about, pumping his shotgun, and ran through the doorway that led out of the stairwell. The giant demon came crashing through the wall after him. It punched and tore at the walls of the corridor in its anger as it charged forward. Walt saw Simon and Sarah up ahead of him running in his direction. Simon was taking aim at the monster with his rifle and Sarah held her revolvers ready in her hands.

Simon's rifle cracked. Walt felt the bullet whiz past him. The sniper's shot was deadly accurate. It pulped the giant demon's right eye inside its socket. The demon screeched, rearing its head back as one of its massive hands slapped over its devastated eye. Blood seeped between its fingers, dripping onto the floor of the corridor. Walt took advantage of the giant demon's pain, skidding to a halt to turn and fire at it again himself. His shotgun boomed as its blast ripped into the flesh of the demon's chest.

The demon took a swipe at him as Walt threw himself from the path of its swing. The demon's claws raked along the corridor wall, slashing a long groove across it. Walt held tight to his shotgun as he turned to run from the monster again. Staying close to it was suicide. With its supernaturally driven strength, a single blow from it would likely end his life or at best leave him crippled on the floor in front of it.

With Walt between her and the giant demon, Sarah held her fire. Simon didn't though. The sniper fired his rifle a second time, taking out the monster's other eye. The giant demon's head snapped sideways as it was left blinded with blood pouring from where its eyes had been.

Walt watched as the demon staggered forward a few more steps and then collapsed onto its knees. He knew he had to finish it. Walt approached the giant demon, careful not to be hit by its flailing arms, and shoved the barrel of his shotgun into its mouth, squeezing the trigger. The giant demon's head exploded in a shower of gore that splattered the walls and floor of the corridor.

"Did Cally get the bomb set?" Walt shouted at Sarah and Simon.

It was Cally who answered him as she came running around the bend of the corridor to join them.

"We're good to go," Cally said. "We've got three minutes until this place is toast."

****

Walt and the others made it outside and were racing down the steps from the building's main entrance as it blew behind them. The explosion lit the night and sent debris spinning away from it into the night. The shockwave knocked them all off their feet but no one was seriously hurt, nothing more than bruises and perhaps wounded pride.

The team wasted no time returning to the Beast and getting back to the Hub. Each of them filed out of the APC tired but with their wounds healed. There were game points to be spent on new weapons, skill upgrades, and stat boosts but all of it seemed hollow. The game was no longer something but to be enjoyed but rather something that *must* be endured and survived. There only way out of it and back to the real world was to complete it.

"Cally, take a look and see what our choices are for the next level," Walt ordered.

"On it, boss man," the young tech answered and disappeared to get the information he had asked for.

"Glad you were able to pull it together," Walt said to Simon. "Without you and that rifle of yours, we'd likely all be dead."

Simon shrugged. "Just doing my part."

"Go on and spend your points," Walt told him. "Something tells me we're going to need everything we've got and then some for the next one."

Simon's coordination/targeting score was already maxed out. He figured boosting his agility would be his best bet and spent his points doing so. As to Sarah, she dumped her points into increasing the damage dealt from by her katana. Walt had a great deal of points built up and spent them all on his health/endurance.

Given how he kept taking hits on each level, it seemed the thing to do.

Cally returned not looking very happy.

"What did you find out?" Walt asked.

"The next level doesn't give us a choice," Cally said with concern in her voice. "The game has just decided we're going up against vampires."

Simon's eyes bugged as he blurted out. "No fragging way!"

Everyone on the team knew that vampires were among the worst of the monsters the game could throw at them. As cliché' as it was, there were few creatures as deadly or as powerful. Usually, things like Vampires were saved for the final level in a game like the one they were trapped in. They were not monsters you ever wanted to go up against if you had a choice.

"Vampires," Sarah sighed, repeating the word.

"Cally, is this next one the final level?" Walt was hopeful that it was.

"One more after it, boss man," Cally informed him.

"Then why vampires?" Sarah looked around at the others. "That's crazy."

"This entire mess is crazy," Walt added. "None of this should be happening."

"But it is," Sarah reminded him. "Let's just be thankful none of us died getting through the last level. Besides, we all know about vampires and how to deal with them. There shouldn't be any unexpected surprises like that giant demon boss that came out of nowhere."

"I still don't like it," Simon said, shaking his head.

"Gear up, everybody," Walt ordered, "the Beast is rolling in five."

Walt exchanged then normal ammo for his shotguns in trade for white phosphorus shells and made sure the magazine in his pistol and his spares for it contained silver bullets. He also selected a tri-barreled stake cannon. It was a large weapon and took to both hands to use, but if used correctly, it could kill lesser vamps with a single shot. Cally loaded up her P-90 with silver rounds too and added several stakes and a wooden knife to what she carried. Sarah spent the final game points she had held in reserve to have the blade of her katana "blessed" and tucked wooden daggers into the tops of her boots. Simon grabbed a couple of UV grenades, some silver-coated .50 caliber rounds for his rifle, an Uzi for close-in defense, and strapped a cross around his neck.

Cally laughed when she saw the cross that the sniper wore.

"You know you have to have faith for that to work, right?" she challenged him.

Simon ignored her jab and turned to Walt. "You're a believer, aren't you?"

"I am," Walt answered.

"Then you should be carrying a cross too," Simon told him.

"My faith and this new ammo are enough for me," Walt said, showing Simon a handful of the new shells he had armed himself with.

"Right," Simon said, clearly doubting what Walt had just said.

"Everyone ready?" Walt asked as the team began to pile into the Beast through the APC's open side door.

"As we'll ever be," Sarah said.

"Okay then." Walt took the seat next to Cally in the driver compartment of the Beast.

Cally cranked up the Beast and drove it out of the Hub onto the next level of the game.

****

The Beast rolled to a stop atop a small hill looking out over the valley below. In the center of the valley was a massive mansion that the vampires they sought were currently using as a place to escape the daylight hours. The game, of course, didn't send the team in during those hours. As Cally killed the APC's engine, the sun was already sinking from the sky and long shadows slithered through the trees of the woods around the hilltop.

"We've got maybe half an hour of sunlight left at best," Walt said. "I suggest we get ourselves a plan and put them to good use."

"I say we just drive the rest of way to the mansion, ram through its front door, and get this over with," Sarah snarled.

"The vampires would see us coming for sure," Cally said. "Even if all of them haven't woken up for the night yet, you can bet they've got some sort of guardians watching out for trouble. We do what you're suggesting and we're as good as dead. They'll see us coming and we'll lose the only advantage we have at the moment—surprise."

"Don't kid yourself, Cally," Simon snorted. "Some of those vamps down there are masters. You can count on it. So they likely already know that we're here or at least that we're coming. They can probably sense us right now."

"We don't know what sort of powers these vamps have, Simon. Every vamp is different. You know that," Walt pointed out. "None of them may be telepathic, precognitive, or anything like that."

"You wanna bet your life on it?" Simon responded.

"Not really," Walt answered. "But we won't know what we're dealing with until we are in the thick of it. We can theorize and guess all we want but that is the truth of it."

"I'm not sure what's worse, the ones with mental powers or the ones with super speed," Sarah commented. "We only thought those werewolves were fast. A speedster vamp will make those wolves seem like they were moving in slow motion."

"What we can count on is that all of them will have super strength, regeneration, and fangs ready to tear out our throats," Walt said.

"That's all great, but I'm not hearing anyone saying anything about having a better plan than my suggestion," Sarah stared at Walt, challenging him.

"I understand how much you want this game to be over with, Sarah. We all feel like that, but charging in there blind is only going to get us killed," Walt told her.

"I agree with Walt," Cally spoke up. "There has to be a better option."

"This thing has a missile sheathed inside its roof." Simon rapped his knuckles against the ceiling of the APC above his seat. "We could use it and blow that place down there apart, force the vamps to come out to us."

Cally was shaking her head. "That wouldn't work, Simon. The missile isn't powerful enough to blow that mansion. Destroy a section of it maybe, sure, but not the whole place. It would just tick the vamps off. It wouldn't drive them out."

"Look, I hate to say it, but our best option is for us to go in on foot," Walt said.

"By the time we made it down this hill and across the valley, the sun will have set," Sarah said, gesturing through the Beast's front window at the sky which continued to get darker with each passing minute.

"Well, sitting here arguing about what to do isn't helping anything," Cally complained, getting frustrated with it all.

"She's right," Walt said. "We need to go on foot and we need to go now. The longer we wait, the more of an edge we give to the vamps."

"Fine." Sarah rose from her seat and moved to slid open the Beast's side door without saying another word to Walt or the others.

"Way to tick *her* off, mate," Simon said, frowning at Walt as he rose to follow after her.

Cally started to get out of the driver's seat but Walt stopped her and shook his head.

"You're not going with us on this one, Cally," he said.

"What? Why? We're all in this together, Walt, now more than ever," Cally protested.

"Exactly," Walt said. "I need you here. If things go south and they likely will, we need the Beast's firepower. By you staying here, we can bring that to the table if we need it."

Understanding dawned in Cally's eyes though she still wasn't happy about being left behind.

"I get it, Walt," Cally told him. "I'll do what you're asking of me, but you better get moving before I change my mind."

Walt smiled at her. "See ya soon then," he said and then followed Sarah and Simon out of the APC.

The night was hot and muggy. Wherever this place was supposed to be, it was summer time. The humidity weighed down on them as the three monster hunters started their trek towards the distant mansion where the vampires waited. Walt wiped sweat from underneath the edge of his combat helmet with the backside of his hand as he walked. He didn't want to die. There was a life outside the game waiting on him if he ever got back to it. Vampires were tough S.O.B.s and nothing that lay ahead of them was going to easy.

Full and bright in the almost cloudless night sky above the moon illuminated the woods with more than enough light to see. Walt wished it would rain. He loved the rain and how it washed the world clean.

Seeing his faraway expression, Sarah whispered, "You with us, Walt?"

Walt nodded, holding his tri-barreled stake gun so tight that his knuckles were white. He had expected Simon to have another breakdown but so far the sniper seemed to be handling this level better than he was. Simon moved with the same cocksure confidence that he had before the game had gone insane and folks had started dying for real in it. Maybe Simon had made his peace with dying. Whatever was going through Simon's head though,

Walt was glad for it. They all needed to be on the top of their game given what they were hunting.

A howl rang out in the darkness nearby. Another followed it. Soon, there were a full-out chorus of the cries coming from all around them and closing in fast.

"Werewolves?" Simon asked.

"I don't think so," Sarah said, shaking her head. "As fragged up as this game is, I don't think even it would cheat that much to take us out. Werewolves and vamps on the same level would be guaranteed kill with how weakened our group is."

"More likely those cries belong to normal wolves under the control of the vampires," Walt agreed. "Let's be ready for them."

Walt slung his stake cannon onto his shoulder by its strap and drew his shotgun from its sheath where the weapon rested on his back. He pumped a round into its chamber with a grim smile parting his lips.

The trio of monster hunters came to a halt, forming a circle that was almost back to back as they watched the trees for movements. Walt saw a pair of amber eyes in the darkness amid the trees watching them in return. Shapes circled the hunters in the darkness, moving quickly careful to stay hidden in the natural cover the woods provided them with. Walt guessed the pack was made up of close to a dozen of the animals though he couldn't be sure. The wolves were gray, he could see that much. Each of them looked to weigh around one hundred pounds based on their size. Their foreheads were wide above long, blunted muzzles. Their lips were pulled back in snarls as they waited on the alpha male among them to give the signal to go after the hunters. A good many times, a wolf would retreat if its prey stood its ground and fought back. These wolves wouldn't though and Walt knew it. They were being goaded on by the controlling force of the vampires that guarded. Each of them would fight to its end in the service of its masters.

One of the wolves sprang forward from the trees, charging at Simon. The sniper's rifle was slung across his back behind his shoulders. He opened up on the animal with the Uzi he carried, emptying half a magazine into it. The wolf shrieked and whined as bullets ripped through its body, rupturing organs and tearing holes in its flesh. Its corpse collapsed a few feet in front of where the sniper stood.

Walt didn't know if it was anger at the death of their pack mate, the smell of fresh blood on the wind, or the will of the vampires controlling them, but the wolves suddenly erupted from the woods as one. They came bounding into the small clearing at the monster hunters, determined to taste their flesh. Holding his ground, Walt's shotgun bucked in his hands as he fired the weapon. A flash of flames like a dragon's breath sprayed from its barrel. The wolf coming at him was hit full on by it. Shots from the shell took chunks of meat from the wolf even as the white phosphorous set the animal ablaze. The wounded wolf rolled about on the ground, leaking blood from its wounds, trying vainly to put out the fires raging all over its body. The flash of Walt's shot shook the charge of the other wolves even as they continued forward, giving the edge to Sarah and Simon. Simon finished emptying his Uzi's magazine at two of the wolves, hosing them both. Their bullet-riddled forms tumbled to into the dirt and stayed there, one dead, one too shot up to do anything but bleed out.

Sarah's revolvers boomed in rapid succession as her thumbs pulled back their hammers and her fingers squeezed their triggers. Her first three shots opened up the skulls of an equal number of wolves, killing them instantly. Even being pushed forward by the will of the vampire controlling them, the shock of the slaughter they had charged into was too much for the wolf pack. They tried to break and run, seeking the cover of the trees but none of the monster hunters were willing to let them go so easily. Simon popped his Uzi's spent magazine, slamming a fresh one home. He brought up the weapon in time to pepper the back of one of the retreating wolves with bullets. The wolf slumped over and didn't move again. Sarah managed five more shots at the retreating pack. Each of them struck its target. The head of one wolf snapped forward on its neck as bullets blew out the rear of its skull. Another severed the spine of a wolf and sent it rolling. By the time they disappeared into the trees, only three of the wolves remained alive.

Simon gave a grunt-like laugh. "Well, that was easy enough."

"They were just animals," Sarah said sadly.

"Yeah, animals that wanted to rip out our throats," Simon huffed, unsure how to take her comment.

"All that matters is that it's over," Walt interrupted the two of them. "The sun has already set and you can bet that everything in this valley knows we're here now. They would have to be deaf not to."

"Nothing we can do about that," Sarah replied.

"I know," Walt said. "Let's get moving."

A few minutes later, the trio of monster hunters reached the edge of the large clearing surrounding the mansion in the valley's center. There were lights on inside many of the mansion's rooms but no sign of guards posted outside it. That worried Walt. He had figured the vamps would make at least one more move at them with some other kind of their servants before opting to get their own immortal, pale hands dirty dispatching a group of three lowly humans.

The team crouched in the bushes near the front of the mansion. Walt traded his shotgun for his stake gun as they got ready to make their move.

"Front door?" Simon whispered.

Walt nodded. There wasn't much point in trying for stealth anymore not after the battle with the wolves.

"Simon, hold back and let Sarah and I take the lead," Walt told the sniper.

"Roger that," Simon answered.

Walt and Sarah burst from the bushes, charging the mansion's front door. Walt didn't even bother trying it. He kicked the door in, nearly taking it completely off its hinges. The door swung inward and he was through it in a heartbeat. Walt took the left and Sarah the right on the other side of door, weapons ready, as they looked around for any vamps who might be waiting to meet them.

The room the front doorway led into was a massive open space. At its rear was a stairway leading up to the mansion's second floor. And that was where the vamps came from. A pale man and woman bounded over the railing that ran the length of the second floor above the room that Sarah and Walt stood in. They hit the floor as gracefully as cats, already moving towards them as their feet hit the floor.

Sarah's revolvers boomed as she engaged the male vampire. Her hands moved like lightning. Even with her speed though, she was only able to get off two shots before the vampire plowed into her. The first put a hole in the vampire's forehead, the second grazing the side of his skull. The vampire ignored both wounds as if it was far beyond feeling pain like a mortal would. The impact for the vampire crashing in her lifted Sarah from her feet and flung her backwards into the wall beside the mansion's front door. Her breath left her lungs in a pained grunt. She would have fallen forward but the vampire was there to catch her. His right hand took her about her throat, shoving her into the wall and holding her there. Sarah kicked at the vampire's knee, trying to break it. Her kick landed firm and hard and would've shattered the knee of a human. It did nothing to the vampire. She continued to struggle against his grip on her as the vampire's cold fingers closed tighter about her throat and forced her head up and around, trying to force her to look into his eyes. Sarah wasn't having it though. With her eyes closed, she yanked a wooden dagger from one of her boots. Its blade sunk into the side of the vampire's throat. Stale, corrupted blood sprayed from where the dagger had entered as she jerked the weapon free. The vampire howled, releasing her. Sarah allowed herself to drop to the floor and brought her knife up into the vampire's groin. The vampire's howl grew high pitch and intensity as she twisted the knife inside of its privates. She rolled away from the vampire, leaving her knife in it as the vampire reached for the weapon's hilt to yank it free of its body. The vampire was staggering as it turned to come after her again. Sarah was ready for it. Her other wooden knife had already been drawn and she rammed through the vampire's sternum into its heart. The vampire shrieked as the poison of the wood in its heart set its body ablaze. It less than a second, the vampire erupted in flames and was gone.

The female vampire came at Walt like a snarling great cat, sure of herself and moving at an inhuman speed that was so fast she seemed to blur as she moved. Walt calmly stood his ground and fired his stake gun. She paid the price for her arrogance as the stake thudded into her chest and she became a ball of raging fire.

"Nice shot," Sarah said, turning to Walt.

"Thanks." He grinned at her. Such a compliment coming from the team's resident gunslinger wasn't to be taken lightly.

Walt and Sarah braced themselves for another attack but the great, open room was quiet.

"Where to?" Sarah asked.

Walt gestured at the stairs. Sarah took the lead starting up them. They reached the second floor and started moving through it room by room in search of more of the vampires. The first two hadn't been masters. Based on how easily they had been dealt with, Walt figured both of them had been recently turned.

A door opened at the far end of the floor. Three vampires emerged from it. They took up defensive positions near the door as another vampire, that was clearly a master, followed them out. The master had long black hair that covered her shoulders. Her eyes glowed red as she looked at the two hunters with contempt.

"You are fools to come here," the master purred.

"Sarah," Walt said.

"I've got the twit," Sarah growled. "You take the others."

Sarah's revolvers came up and thundered as the male vampires charged at them. She didn't aim for any of them though;

she was aiming at the master. The master moved with impossible speed and agility as the bullets from Sarah's guns streaked through the spot where she had been standing only a fraction of a second before. The master sprung onto the ceiling and scampered across it above the other vampires, passing them as they came at Walt to fling herself onto Sarah. Sarah screamed as the master landed on her and the two of them together crashed through the railing of the second floor, toppling downward to the first.

"Sarah!" Walt screamed as he watched them fall, but there was nothing he could do. He had three vamps of his own to deal with. Firing his stake gun, he sent one of the three charging vamps to Hell with a shot to its heart. The other two reached him before he could fire his weapon's last stake. One of them snatched the gun from his hands, crushing it effortlessly in its grip before hurling the broken weapon aside. The second vampire swung a fist at Walt's head. Walt ducked the swing, moving past the vampire at a full-out run. He unsheathed his shotgun as he went and brought it about to fire point blank into the vampire that had destroyed his stake gun. Flames spurted from the shotgun's barrel, washing over the vampire as the blast knocked him a step backwards, leaving a ragged, gaping hole in his chest. The chest wound began to heal itself instantly but not even the vampire's supernatural-level regeneration could keep up with the white phosphorus that burnt away his flesh. The vampire howled in pain as Walt fired again. He went for a headshot this time at point-blank range. The vampire tried to lash out and knock the barrel of the shotgun away from his face, but the pain he was in slowed him too much. His hand struck the weapon after it had discharged its deadly contents. The vampire's skull blew apart from the blast as

Walt's shotgun went flying from his hands to bounce off the wall nearby. It landed far out of his reach.

Immortal or not, the vampire was dead. The white phosphorus combined with the loss of its head sealed its fate. It wouldn't be coming back. Walt still had the last of the three male vampires to deal with though. He was down to just his sidearm which was next to useless against something like a vampire. Walt moved to yank it from the holster on his hip as the vamp came at him. It tackled him like a football player, taking him to the floor beneath it. The vampire's fangs plunged towards his neck as it held his arms tight against the floor. Walt closed his eyes, accepting his fate, but instead of feeling the fangs sink into him, the vampire's blood splattered over him as a bullet entered the side of its head.

"Move!" he heard Simon shout from the first floor below. The sniper had entered the mansion managed a nigh impossible shot that had just saved his life. The vampire on top of him was far from dead but it was stunned. Walt shoved the vamp from him and leaped to his feet, running for the stairs. He heard the vampire heave itself to its feet and lunge after him, but Simon's rifle cracked again twice in rapid succession. Glancing over his shoulder as he ran, Walt saw Simon's two shots blow out the vamp's knees. The vampire went sprawling onto the floor, its outstretched hand reaching vainly for him.

Walt went down the steps of the stairs two, sometimes even three at a time. He desperately needed a weapon. He still held onto his pistol but he needed something with a bigger bang. As he hit the bottom of the stairs, Simon was there waiting for him.

"Sarah?" Walt asked.

"No sign of her," the sniper answered gruffly, tossing Walt his Uzi.

"It's not much, but it's loaded up with silver," Simon told him as Walt caught the weapon one-handed.

Walt holstered his pistol, gripping the Uzi with both hands. "Sarah and the master should be down here," he said.

"I didn't see them as I came in," Simon assured him. "If they were here, they're gone now."

"We've got to find them," Walt barked, his eyes scanning the large room for any clue as to where they had disappeared to.

"I don't think that'll be a problem," Simon croaked, gesturing at the mansion's open front door.

The master vampire came strolling through it, dragging Sarah alongside her by a handful of Sarah's hair.

"Hello, boys," she said, grinning at them, showing her fangs.

"Frag you!" Simon shouted and took a shot at her with his rifle.

She made no move to dodge the incoming round. The master vampire stood her ground and allowed it blow a ragged hole in her guts. Her intestines spilled out of her in thick purple stands. She didn't even so much as flinch. Ever so calmly, she reached down to run a finger through her own ruptured guts and then raised the blood-smeared finger to her lips to lick it clean.

The two monster hunters stared at her in horror. Walt snapped out of his shock first, leveling the barrel of the Uzi he held at the master vampire. He squeezed its trigger and held it tight. Again, she made no move to avoid the fire coming at her. Her body twitched and jerked as the silver rounds ripped at her flesh.

When Walt's Uzi clicked empty, she laughed. "My turn?"

Without waiting for an answer, the master vampire surged forward, knocking Walt from her path as she went after Simon. Walt bounced across the floor of the room as she grabbed Simon around the throat with her right hand lifted him effortlessly. Walt heard Simon's neck snap as the master vampire broke it with a simple flick of her thumb and pointer finger. She dropped the sniper's corpse and turned to glance at Walt where he was beginning to pull himself back onto his feet.

"This is no longer a game, Walt," the master vampire yelled in a voice that was not her own. "This is vengeance!"

Walt's heart froze inside his chest as he recognized the voice that came from the master vampire's lips. It couldn't be, but it was. Walt supposed it didn't matter. He was dead anyway. She was far too powerful to stop with just his pistol.

The master vampire's voice became her own again as she approached him. Walt made no move to flee. He had seen how fast she was.

"Who are you?" Walt asked, seeking confirmation of what he already knew to be true.

"I am your death," the master vampire hissed, baring her fangs as she snarled at him.

"I don't think so," Sarah shouted, coming out of nowhere to ram a broken piece of wooden railing from the stairs into the master vampire's heart.

"No!" the master vampire shrieked and then exploded into flames. Within seconds, there was nothing left of her but ash that drifted about in the air where her body had burnt away.

Walt fell forward onto his knees as Sarah rushed over to him.

"You okay?" she asked with deep concern in her voice.

"I'm fine," Walt rasped. "We have to get back to the Hub as soon as possible. I know what's going on with the game now."

Sarah shifted about where she knelt as his statement hit her like clinched fist knocking the wind out of her.

"What?" she stammered. "How?"

"Not now," Walt told her. "We'll talk when we're all together. Cally needs to hear this too."

"Okay," Sarah reluctantly agreed and radioed Cally to bring the Beast down into the valley to pick them up. When she was done, she turned to Walt.

"Should we bury him or something?" Sarah asked.

"No point," Walt said, shrugging sadly. "This level and everything in it will dematerialize as soon as we're gone from it."

"That's really sad," Sarah commented as she stared at the sniper's body.

"At least he died fast," Walt told her. "Poor Brent … Only God knows how long he burned before death claimed him."

The Beast drove up to them and stopped a few feet from where they stood. A second later, Cally slid the APC's side door open. She took one look at the two of them and knew Simon was gone before she ever noticed the sniper's body where it lay nearby.

"Come on," Walt said, entering the Beast and shoving past Cally, "we have to get to the Hub."

Cally gave Sarah a questioning look as the gunslinger followed Walt inside.

"Something happened out there," Sarah said. "I don't know what, but Walt thinks he knows what's going on with the game now."

"Really?" Cally asked.

"Really," Sarah said.

****

The Beast rolled into the garage that made up the front section of the Hub as its exterior door closed behind it. Walt was out of his seat and moving like a man possessed as soon as the APC came to a stop.

Sarah and Cally caught up to him at the central control terminal that allowed access to all the Hub's systems and that the team used to select their course for the next level.

"That level should have been the last one," Walt said as he heard them walking up behind him. "But it's not. Someone has rewritten the game for there to be one more."

"Whoa, Walt, slow down." Sarah put a hand on his shoulder. "What do you mean someone rewrote the game? That's not possible, is it?"

"It might be," Cally said. "But the level of hacking it would take … wow."

"Someone did rewrite the game," Walt told them. "Someone has completely altered it. They've removed the safeties that keep us from experiencing biofeedback in the real world when we die in here. That's why the others are dead out there."

"Walt, you can't be serious?" Sarah argued. "Who would do such a thing?"

He stared at them both almost as if he were reluctant to tell them what he had apparently figured out.

"If you know who is behind all this, you have to tell us, Walt," Cally demanded.

"Chad," Walt said flatly. "It's Chad."

Cally staggered at the name Walt had spoken. She nearly fell to the floor of the Hub but managed to catch herself by reaching out to cling to the side of the central control terminal.

"It can't be," Cally wailed. "He wouldn't … He couldn't do this to us."

"He has the skills, Cally," Walt said. "And the motive. He's hated all of us ever since we kicked him out of the group for bending the rules in here."

"That's a pretty hefty accusation, Walt," Sarah said. "The guy was a jerk and cheater but that doesn't mean he's a murderer."

"It all fits, Sarah, and you know it does." Walt stared her down. "This is the first time we've all played since we kicked him out and that was weeks ago. He's had more than enough time to set all this up and let us upload ourselves into this … trap he's set for us."

"I get that the guy was upset, Walt. I do but who kills people for just kicking them out of a game?" Sarah argued.

"It's more than that," Cally spoke up. "He … he tried to rape me, Sarah."

Sarah stared at Cally in utter shock. It took her a moment to find the words to speak again. "What in the holy devil do you mean he tried to rape you?"

"He did, Sarah," Cally answered with tears welling up in her eyes to slide over the curves of her cheeks. "Chad did a lot more in here than just bend the rules in his favor. He added a room to the Hub and lured me into it. His hands were all over me, Sarah, and he wouldn't take no for an answer. If Walt hadn't discovered the room and showed up when he did …" Cally sobbed.

"You knew about this?" Sarah whirled on Walt. "And you didn't tell any of us about it?"

"Cally asked me not to and we all voted to kick Chad out anyway." Walt raised his hands, open-palmed in a gesture that begged for mercy from the gunslinger's growing rage. "I tried to get Cally to file charges against him in the real world, but what else could I do?"

"And did you?" Sarah turned to Cally. "Did you file charges on the creep?"

Cally nodded. "I did. Last I heard, his parents had bailed him out."

"That mother fragger," Sarah growled, clenching her hands into fists.

"Think about it, Sarah," Walt urged the gunslinger. "Once he got out, you can bet he wanted some payback on all of us. I would wager it didn't take long for him to decide to take us out one by one in here. If we all died from something that looked like a glitch or malfunction in the game, then there would be no one left to testify against him out there in the real world. It would be his word against that of a dead girl's. With the sort of lawyers his parents' money can buy, he'd be off the hook, free and clear for what he tried to do to Cally."

"That bastard." Sarah was so angry she was shaking as she stepped away from Walt.

"Walt," Cally said, still sobbing, "you said there was one level left."

"Right," Walt replied. "Just one according to the level layout on the terminal, and it's not one that is supposed to exist so there's no data on what's waiting for us on it."

"So that's it then?" Sarah stared at Walt. "All we can do is face the bastard in here and hope he hasn't rigged the game to the point that we don't have a chance of stopping him?"

"That pretty much sums it up. Yeah," Walt said.

"Chad is one of the best hackers I've ever seen," Cally wiped at her tears, "but I don't think even he could change the rules in here to the point that we had no chance at all."

"I guess we better hope that you're right," Sarah grunted.

"She is," Walt stated flatly. "But there is something we can do to stack the odds in our favor."

"And what would that be?" Sarah demanded.

"Chad may be a blasted good hacker, but let's not forget that we have a hacker of our own," Walt said, gesturing at Cally.

"What?" Cally flinched. "I don't know that I can ..."

"You can, Cally," Walt assured her. "Everything you need is right here in the Hub. You know as well as I do there are cheat codes out there that folks with less integrity than us use all the time. I'm willing to wager that you know some of them too."

Cally didn't bother to claim that she didn't. "Are you sure about this, Walt? What if I just mess things up more?"

"You won't," Walt said. "I have faith in you, kid. You can do this."

"Okay," Cally said, nodding. "It'll take some time though."

Walt pulled out the seat at the terminal station for her. "Then you better get started."

****

Walt and Sarah left Cally alone to do her work. The time limit for the Hub had been suspended to a degree. Like everything else in the game, it had gone wonky too. Walt opened the door to the team's primary arsenal and stepped inside it.

"I can't believe you didn't tell us about Chad," Sarah challenged him, following Walt inside.

"What was there to tell, Sarah?" Walt said. "Cally begged me not to let anyone know. We kicked the guy out of the group and she agreed to file charges in the real world. It took a lot of pressure from me just to get her to do that. She's not you."

"The guy was always a jerk." Sarah frowned. "I'm just saying it would have been nice to know he was a monster too. I would have liked to—"

"To what, Sarah?" Walt whirled on her. "Watch Brent kill him and then get sent to jail? Because we both know that's what would have happened. Brent loved Cally more than any of us. There's no way he would have let something like what Chad did go unanswered … And he would have paid the price for his vengeance too."

"I get it, Walt," Sarah told him. "I understand how you handled it and why. It doesn't make any of it any easier to deal with though."

"Tell me about it," Walt agreed. "On the upside, since Chad has brought this fight to us, you're going to get your shot at him and now, it will be self-defense."

"I'm worried about this next level," Sarah admitted. "I don't like going in blind."

"Nothing we can do about that," Walt said. "Only God knows what sort of horrors Chad has dreamed up for us on it. You can bet he'll be there though. The guy was always a braggart and show off. He loved having an audience for everything he did. Looking back, I think he even wanted to get caught doing what he tried to do to Cally; he just didn't expect me to find him and his secret little room as quickly I did."

"You've always been a good leader, Walt," Sarah told him.

"Have I?" Walt stared at her. "How many of us are dead, Sarah? Simon, Brent, and Lee have all paid the price for me allowing Chad to blindside us."

"You couldn't possibly have had any idea that Chad was going to do this, Walt," Sarah argued. "The guy may be a sicko and crazy, but what he's done to this game, trapping us in it to kill us one at a time, that's above and beyond even for him."

"I let them down, Sarah," Walt confessed, the guilt he felt eating away at him from the inside. "I should have done more the second this all started. If I had, maybe at least Brent and Simon would be alive right now."

"You did all you could," Sarah assured him. "Without you leading us through this madness like you have, we might all be dead already."

"Look, rehashing all this isn't doing either of us any good," Walt said. "We know who we're up against now and we need to get ready to face him. Nothing we do or say at this point will bring the others back but we can sure make Chad pay for what he's done."

"Oh trust me," Sarah said, grinning, "I am looking forward to that."

Walt moved about the rows of weapons, gearing up for the level that lay ahead of them. He sheathed two shotguns on his back, one loaded with white phosphorous shells and the other an automatic loaded with heavy slugs. Clipping two grenades to his belt, he also traded out his standard sidearm for a fully automatic machine pistol with an extended magazine. He didn't feel like that was enough for this one so he grabbed an AK-47 as well.

"That's a lot of weapons," Sarah said, eyeing him. "You sure you got enough?"

"Like you said, going in blind is dangerous." Walt readied his AK-47. "I want to be prepared for whatever we run into out there. Aren't you taking anything extra?"

Sarah shook her head. "My revolvers and sword are all I need, Walt. They're my thing and I like to think I am pretty darn good with them."

The two of them walked out of the arsenal and headed to the Beast to wait there for Cally. Walt noticed Sarah continued to look at him strangely.

"What's up, Sarah?" he finally caved in and asked her. "I'm not an idiot. I've known you long enough to know when something's wrong."

"Why does it have to be that something's wrong, Walt?" Sarah said.

Walt shrugged. He didn't have an answer to that one.

She stepped into his path as they reached the Beast, preventing him from entering the APC's open side door.

"What are you—?" Walt started but Sarah never gave him the chance to finish. One of her hands grabbed him by the back of his head and pulled his face towards her. Her lips met his as her other around slid around him to pull their bodies close. At first, Walt tried to pull away but he surrendered quickly and lost himself in the kiss that they shared. He was breathless when Sarah released him and pulled away.

"I've wanted to do that for a long, long time, Walt," Sarah told him. "I just have never had the courage to until right now."

"I can't believe you'd be afraid of anything, Sarah," he stammered. "Much less something like that."

"Walt, if we live through this…" Sarah started, but it was his turn to cut her off.

"Yeah." Walt rested his hands on her shoulders. "I promise."

Sarah nodded. "Then I reckon we both have another reason to stay alive out there."

Walt laughed. "We sure do."

"Ahem!" both of them heard Cally behind them. "I've finished with the cheat codes."

"Uh …right …" Walt's cheeks flushed red as Cally looked the two of them over.

"It's about time," Cally said to Sarah.

"The cheat codes?" Walt blurted out before the situation could get any more awkward.

"I rigged up one for each of us," Cally told him. "It was the best I could do. Each of us has one special thing we can use on this next level."

Cally turned to face him. "Walt, I gave you a code called One Shot, One Kill. When you activate it, whatever you shoot will die. Doesn't matter how powerful or what it is, the damage you do to it will be lethal. Just don't waste it on something stupid, okay?"

"I won't," Walt said. "Thank you."

"And what about me?" Sarah asked gleefully.

"I was able to hook you up with a short burst of super speed. The chest is called Hyper. Once you activate it, you'll have a few seconds in which you'll be able to move faster than a master vampire. I figured that sort of cheat fit your style," Cally answered her.

"And you would be right," Sarah replied, smiling at the young tech.

"What about you, Cally? What did you rig up for yourself?" Walt asked.

"The two I rigged up for you guys were the best I had time to get," Cally admitted. "I had to go with a very basic one for myself. It's called Respawn. Unlike the ones I gave the two of you, it's automatic and doesn't have to be turned on. If I die out there, it should bring me back at the exact spot and time where I die. Whether or not it'll work given how Chad's altered the game, I don't know, but like I said, it was all I had time to rig up."

"Here's hoping it works," Sarah said grimly.

"Just don't count on it, Cally," Walt warned her. "I don't want you taking unnecessary risks out there because you think that code will save you."

"Trust me, I won't," Cally promised.

"I guess that's it then, huh?" Walt stepped into the Beast. "We better get going."

"Couldn't agree more," Sarah said, taking her usual seat in the rear of the Beast as Walt and Cally headed up into the driver's compartment. Cally slid into the driver's seat and Walt plopped into the seat next to her.

"Take us out," Walt ordered.

Cally cranked up the Beast and drove it out of the Hub.

****

The Beast rolled to a stop amid the sand dunes. The sun was high and bright in the sky above. Its rays scorched the earth beneath it. The sky was blue and cloudless. No matter which way one looked, there was only a sea of sand that stretched onward into the horizon.

"Where is this place?" Cally asked.

"If you don't know, how the frag are we supposed to?" Sarah shot back at her.

"Ladies," Walt said, bringing an end to their bickering.

"I'm just saying what sort of monster actually likes the sun?" Sarah complained, sulking in the rear of the Beast.

"Could be where a mummy would hang out?" Cally giggled.

"Mummies are so … dated." Sarah got out of her seat. "Chad was a tasteless bastard but even he wouldn't send mummies against us."

Sarah slid the Beast's side door open and leaped out into the sand. She turned back to glance at the others. "You coming?"

Walt sighed and unfastened his seat belt. Cally followed him out after Sarah.

"Dang, it's hot out here," Walt commented. Sweat had already formed on his skin and was beginning to seep through his clothes under his combat armor.

"I don't see Chad letting us wander around out here long," Sarah said. "The guy never could stand to wait for anything."

"Simon would have loved this." Cally looked around at the sand. "He always wanted to play a desert mission."

"Is that a sniper thing?" Sarah chuckled.

Cally shrugged.

"I feel like we're missing something really bloody obvious here, guys," Walt said.

"You're being paranoid," Sarah told him.

"Don't knock it. Me being paranoid has saved us a bunch of times," Walt reminded her.

"He's got a point," Cally said. "And I think he's right. We're all strung pretty tight right now with everything. Whatever Chad has planned for us here could be staring us in the face and we might miss it as clouded as we by our emotions at the moment."

"When did you get all cold-blooded and logical?" Sarah flashed a wry grin.

"Watching your friends die because of you really messes you up," Cally answered.

"Whoa, kid." Walt stepped to place a hand on Cally's shoulder. "This isn't your fault. None of it is. This is all on Chad and has been since the get-go."

"Thanks, Walt," Cally said, meeting his eyes. "I appreciate that."

"It's the truth," Walt told her firmly.

"Uh, guys," Sarah called to them, pointing into the distance, "what's that?"

Walt shielded his eyes as best he could against the harsh sun and looked in the direction she was pointing in. Squinting, he could just barely make out that something was moving out there. It took him a moment to realize that what he was seeing was actually the sand itself rising and shifting as if something was beneath it.

"Worms," Walt muttered, a shiver running along his spine.

"Or some kind of crawlers," Sarah added.

How could I have missed something so obvious? Walt thought. *An environment like this is perfect for any kind of underground monster that Chad could dream up.*

"Everybody back in the Beast!" Walt shouted, already springing into motion and running for the APC.

The three of them had wandered a small distance from the vehicle as they had been talking. It was close but that small distance seemed like it was leagues away now. Whatever the monsters under the sand were, they were fast. They closed in with blinding speed, shooting along like missiles that flung sand into the air above where they traveled.

Cally had been the closest to the Beast. She and Sarah reached it at the same time. Both of them stood just inside its side door, looking out at him as he ran. Walt's legs pumped under him and his muscles ached as he pushed them to their limits and beyond. The adrenaline flowing through him sharpened his senses, making the rumbling and shaking of the ground behind him feel even closer than he thought it might be. He saw Sarah reach to grab a Winchester from the small stash of backup weapons aboard the Beast. She braced the rifle against the side of the door and took aim at whatever was chasing after him. The rifle cracked as its barrel flashed. Walt heard an utterly inhuman noise that was half-shriek, half-hiss as the bullet struck its target. The noise threw off the rhythm of his stride. His left foot came down at an angle, almost breaking his ankle, and he went down, rolling over the sand carried onward by momentum. When he came to a stop, he had rolled to where he was facing the monster that was after him. Walt had expected to see the head of a giant worm or an open mouth sprouting tentacles to grab at him. What he saw though was a monster like something straight out of a nightmare. It was humanoid shaped and towered over him, standing close to eight feet in height. The creature had six arms, three on each side of its body. Its eyes were bulbous like an insect's and protruded from the sides of its head. In the spots where its ears should have been were sunken holes. Its two primary arms ended in crab-like pincers. The other four of its six arms ended a set of three gleaming claws that looked sharp enough to slice through steel. Thick muscles bulged on its arms and legs. The tiniest stump of a tail lay was visible between its legs. The thing opened its mouth, showing him the jagged teeth that lined it, as it gave a hiss of rage. Sarah's shot had taken away a chunk of its right shoulder and black blood ran in rivulets over the top two arms on that side of its body.

Walt didn't waste any time on words expressing his shock. Realizing he had managed to keep a hold on his AK-47, he jerked the barrel of the rifle up towards the monster and squeezed the weapon's trigger. The bullets smacked into the monster standing over him. They blew ragged holes in its body, leaving gaping exit holes in their wake. The monster shrieked, a high-pitched sound of agony, and stumbled backwards before collapsing onto the sand. It lay there in a growing pool of its own blood. Unfortunately, it wasn't alone.

Dozens more of the monsters sprang up from the sand all around the Beast, blocking Walt's path to the heavily armored vehicle. He scrambled to his feet as one the monsters came at him. For all its speed beneath the sand, its movements were awkward and slower above it. Walt hosed the monster with a burst of rounds that sent it reeling away from him.

"Walt!" he heard Sarah shout from inside the doorway of the Beast. Most of the monsters were beginning to converge on the APC. Sarah worked the lever of the Winchester she held, firing one shot after another at the creatures. She splattered one's brains, blew out another's chest in an explosion of gore, and killed several more in the time it took for him to get moving and cover a third of the distance that lay between him and the Beast.

Cally was shooting too. The young tech had drawn her sidearm and was busy emptying its magazine into the approaching creatures. Not all of her shots found their targets like Sarah's but she still managed to wound two or three of the monsters, helping Sarah hold them at bay.

There had been no information on this level available in the Hub. No clear mission or objective that would signal its end. As thus, there was no means of knowing just how many of these creatures they were up against in this desert. Was there merely this pack or were the numbers of the monsters more like those of an unending zombie horde? Walt was at a loss as to what to do. Should they stand their ground and try to wipe out the buggers or hightail it the heck out of this place? All he knew for sure was that whatever these monsters were, they wouldn't be the only ones waiting for them. They were far too easy to kill despite their numbers and apparent strength.

Walt jerked away from a pincer that snapped at him. Cursing that he had allowed one of the things to get in too close, he spun his rifle around in his hands, shifting it into being a melee weapon. Walt rammed the butt of the rifle into the monster's face. The blow appeared to stun the creature but not really do it any serious harm. The time it bought though allowed Walt to sprint away before the monster could make another grab at him.

"Come on!" Sarah yelled at him. "We can't hold these things off forever, ya know?"

"Coming, honey!" Walt shouted back at her as he ran.

Sarah was scowling as he mowed down the last three creatures between him and the Beast with a series of well-controlled bursts. She moved aside to let him as he leaped through the open side door to join her and Cally.

"I think we've had enough of these guys already," Cally shouted, heading for the driver's compartment.

Sarah slammed the door closed, leaning against it as Walt popped the spent magazine from his rifle and shoved a fresh one into it.

Pincers pounded the door and claws raked against metal as the monsters tried to force their way into the vehicle.

"Cally!" Walt screamed.

The Beast's engine roared to life as Cally fired it up. Her foot shoved the accelerator to the floor and the APC lurched forward, building speed as it went. A few of the creatures were unlucky enough to be in its path as it got moving. The Beast plowed through and over them, crushing them to little more than wet smears that stained the sand black.

"Frag!" Walt smashed a balled -up fist into the wall of the Beast's rear compartment. It hurt like the devil but it helped him to control his anger. "We should have known those things would be out there under the sand. How could we be so stupid?"

"We all made it out alive," Sarah told him. "I would call that a win."

Walt looked over at the gunslinger and saw her grinning at him.

"I suppose you're right," Walt admitted. "It could have been worse."

"I am. No doubt about it, Walt," Sarah replied, laughing.

"Where to?" Cally called out to them from the forward compartment where she sat in the driver seat of the APC.

"Anywhere but here," Walt told her.

"Roger that," Cally answered.

****

Walt was thankful none of them had been hurt or worse in their conflict with the sand creatures. He was also thankful for the APC's air conditioning. The heat had been horrid and unlike anything he had ever felt. It had made sense when Cally told them that whatever this level was, it wasn't set on Earth. They were on an alien planet. When he asked how she knew that, Cally had pointed at the twin blazing suns, high in the sky through the Beast's forward window. Walt figured he was an idiot for not noticing something such a large detail about their current environment himself but honestly, his entire being was focused on finding Chad and ending the bastard.

"Pretty freaky, huh?" Sarah asked him, moving up from the Beast's rear compartment to lean over the back of his seat.

"Yeah," Walt agreed, only half paying attention to her.

Cally drove the Beast through the desert sand, trying to figure out where to go. Since there was no road and no mission parameters, she really didn't have a clue.

Suddenly, they all felt the Beast enter transit as if it were making a jump back to the Hub.

"What the …?" Cally blurted out, slamming on the APC's brakes as the APC was gone from the desert in the blink of an eye to reappear in a large, open bay that reminded her of scenes she had seen on TV and in games of a hangar aboard a starship.

"We ain't on that planet anymore," Sarah commented. "Chad's brought us to him."

Cally was nodding. "I'd say that's a good guess. Odds are he was watching our battle with those creatures from up here."

"Up here?" Walt asked.

"Look around, boss," Cally said. "We're clearly onboard some kind of spacecraft."

Walt paused to do as she had suggested. The large, open area contained several small craft that certainly looked to be spaceships of some kind. "Right," he said, feeling like an idiot again.

Shaking his head to clear it and trying to get a grip on their situation, Walt held tight the AK-47 resting in his lap. The weapon brought him comfort.

The trio of monster hunters exited the Beast. Cally secured it as the others readied their weapons.

"Welcome!" Chad's voice boomed from all around them.

"Chad!" Walt yelled. "Come out and face us, you coward!"

Laughter echoed throughout the hangar bay as Chad responded, "Oh, I'll do just that in moment, but first, I have some friends I'd like you to meet."

A door at the far end of the hangar bay dilated open to allow the zombified remains of Brent, Simon, and Lee to enter. Simon's head dangled at an unnatural angle atop his broken neck, leaning to the left. Brent's skin was mostly gone and black coils of smoke drifted upwards from his still-smoldering body. His eye sockets were empty, hollow spaces, the orbs inside long burnt away. Lee had a hole that went all the way through his body from where either he or Chad had removed the weapon that the werewolf had impaled him with. All three of them charged at their former teammates, yellow eyes blazing and their lips parted in snarls that showed their teeth.

"You sick freak!" Sarah shouted. "How could you?"

But then there was no time to do anything but fight and try to survive.

Brent came straight at Walt, a towering juggernaut of muscle and power even dead. Walt hesitated for a fraction of a second too long, allowing Brent to reach him. The big man made a grab for the AK-47 Walt held. His huge hands clasped onto the weapon, jerking it free of Walt's hold on it. Brent grunted as the muscles of his arms bulged and he snapped the rifle in half. Walt was back-pedaling away from what was left of his former friend, trying to wrap his mind around the fact that this thing wasn't trying to kill him wasn't Brent.

Cally didn't have any such hold-ups as Lee charged at her. She yanked her pistol free of its holster and brought it up in a two-handed grip at the zombie. The pistol cracked four times in rapid succession. Her first hurried shot missed Lee completely. Her second slammed grazed his shoulder without any real effect. Giving up on scoring a headshot as Lee drew closer to her with each step, she changed her angle of fire. Her third and fourth rounds smacked into his chest, tearing through it and breaking his momentum. Lee made a sickening, gurgling noise as he vomited blood across the hangar at her. Cally dodged the blood and let out a squeal of terror as she saw that the metal floor where it had landed was melting. She realized that Chad had done more than just bring their friends back to life; he had "upgraded" them too.

Simon and Sarah faced each other like true warriors. As Simon had approached her, the flesh of his arms had solidified into blades of bone that the sniper moved about as if they were swords. Out of respect for his memory, Sarah had drawn her katana and decided to meet him at what she considered a fair fight. They circled each other, both looking for a weakness or an opportune moment in which to strike. It was Simon who made the first move. One of his sword-like arms swept through the air in a wide arc as he went for her neck. Sarah easily blocked the strike with her katana and countered with one of her own. The blade of her katana raked across Simon's abdomen, opening it up and spilling purple, blood-smeared strands of his intestines onto the floor of the hangar. Simon came at her again only to be tripped up by his own guts. Their chords got tangled about his legs and feet, sending him crashing over. Simon hacked at them wildly with his arms, slashing himself free. His arms cut deep grooves in his legs as he did so but none so bad that he couldn't stagger back to his feet. Sarah was there waiting as he rose up. She lashed out with her katana, taking the sniper's head from his shoulders. It bounced across the hangar as a geyser of black blood sprayed from the top of what remained of his neck. His headless body toppled to the floor once more as Sarah stood looking down at it. Waves of nausea washed over her from the smell of Simon's exposed, hacked up, and ruptured guts but she fought them down, willing them away. With Simon finished, Sarah looked around to see where she was needed next.

Walt's retreat from Brent didn't save him. The big man moved with a speed that Walt wouldn't have thought possible to lunge at him. Brent's burnt and fleshless arms wrapped about him, lifting him from the floor in a bear hug. Walt gritted his teeth against the crushing pressure Brent was inflicting on his ribs. His arms were pinned to his sides by Brent's so that he couldn't reach for a new weapon to use against the dead man. Walt's legs kicked as the pressure grew even more intense. He looked into Brent's empty sockets, hoping to see a trace of his former friend inside the monster that held him. There was none to be found. Walt was on the verge of passing out from the pain and lack of air as Sarah came running up behind Brent to sink her katana through his right knee. As she yanked the blade free, having done the damage she had intended to do, Brent's mangled knee gave out him. The giant released Walt falling to the floor of the hangar. Walt flopped onto the floor near Brent, gasping for breath.

Brent whirled about, trying to come to his feet and failing. His efforts finished shattering the knee Sarah had stabbed. The giant reeled sideways, catching himself to remain in a kneeling position instead of collapsing back to the floor. He made a grab for Sarah but she easily sidestepped his attempt and struck again with her sword. Brent's outstretched arm was severed from his body at its elbow by the blade of her katana. Roaring in anger, Brent reared his head back. Sarah's blade flickered through the air once more, ending the giant's unlife by taking his head.

Walt had recovered and was on his feet. He stared at Sarah as she stood over Brent's body.

"It had to be done," he said, trying to comfort her. "It wasn't really Brent."

"It wasn't really Simon either but somehow that doesn't make seem any easier," Sarah told him.

Their attention was drawn to Cally's battle with the last of their dead friends as she screamed out in utter horror and pain. Lee had tackled her, taking the young tech to the floor beneath him. His teeth were snapping at her face in bestial fury as Cally fought to keep them from tearing into her. Both her hands were pressed against Lee's face and throat as he relentlessly tried to get at her.

Walt drew one of his shotguns from where it was sheathed on his back but knew the weapon was useless in helping Cally. Any shot he fired at Lee would hit the young tech too. Thankfully, Sarah was already moving to help her.

Sprinting across the hangar, Sarah came up behind Lee, opening up his back with a swipe of katana. Lee spun to come at so fast that Sarah, even as fast as she was, lost her footing avoiding him. She thudded onto the floor, her katana bouncing out of her grip. Lee crawled over her downed body, leaking blood-tainted saliva from his hungry lips. Sarah felt his cold hands on her, shoving her down and trying to get a better hold on her as Lee's teeth closed on her arm. Sarah grimaced as they broke her skin and dug into her flesh. She channeled the pain into newfound strength as she rolled, flinging Lee off of her. Sarah rose up into a combat stance as Lee sprang at her again. Her right hand whammed into his throat with a blow that would have killed Lee if he had been alive. She followed it up with a flat-palmed strike to his nose with her left, snapping Lee's head back. He staggered away from her, apparently stunned by the combined blows. Lee recovered in the span of a heartbeat though and lashed out at her, the fingers of his left hand catching where his teeth had torn into her arm. The cold fingers sank deep into the wound, sending blood spurting from it. Sarah cried out, knocking his hand away.

Cally's pistol cracked twice as she put two rounds into the back of Lee's skull. His body jerked, tensing up, as brain matter and fragments of bone exploded out from the exit wounds the bullets left in his forehead as they ripped through it. Lee managed to turn around to look at Cally before he fell over and didn't move again.

The trio of monster hunters formed a defensive circle waiting to see what Chad was going to throw at them next. They didn't have to wait long. Another door on the far side of the hangar bay opened and a *thing* born of the darkest and sickest nightmares emerged from it. It stood seven feet tall, its skin translucent, and its eyes glowing an eerie shade of pale blue.

"Did you guys miss me?" the thing asked as it sauntered unhurriedly towards them.

"Chad?" Walt asked.

"Who else?" The thing tried to smile, stretching the malformed muscles of its face into a sick, mockery of the human expression.

"I must say, I didn't expect any of you to get this far." The thing that was Chad laughed. "But I am rather glad you did, especially you, Cally. We have some unfinished business that needs attending to."

A long, pointed tongue slipped from between the thing that was Chad's lips to lick perversely at the air around them.

"You bastard!" Cally shouted, sweeping her pistol up to take aim at the monster. Chad's right arm elongated as it stretched outward with blinding speed. Its fingers closed around the barrel of Cally's pistol before she could even squeeze the weapon's trigger and took it from her hands. Chad's arm retracted as quickly as it had stretched. He raised the pistol to his face, sniffing at it.

"You always did smell like heaven, Cally," Chad purred, his glowing blue eyes focused on the young tech.

"Speed," Sarah whispered the word, activating the cheat code Cally had rigged up for her. The next instant, she was moving. Sarah had closed the distance between her and Chad so fast it looked to Walt like she had teleported to stand directly beside him. She moved about him, the blade of her katana flashing through the air too many times for Walt to even try to count. She slashed open Chad's chest, cut away his legs, took chunks of his strange flesh and bone from the sides of his skull, and finally rammed the sword's blade directly through his heart as if she were staking a vampire. Chad's mangled form slumped to the floor on its knees before her.

"How was that for some payback, you mother fragger?" Sarah spat at Chad, feeling her burst of speed run its course and come to an end.

"Sarah! Get out of there!" Walt yelled at the gunslinger but before he had even finished shouting the words, Chad had completely healed the staggering amount of damage she had done to him and leaped upwards at her. His hands caught Sarah by her arms, holding them in place as the long, pointed tongue he had shown off to Cally thrust from between his lips to stab into the center of Sarah's forehead. There was sucking noise as the tongue became bloated and full of Sarah's cerebral fluid and small pieces of her brain. Sarah's body twitched and spasmed, her eyes opened wide in shock and horror as she died.

Chad swallowed what he had taken from her and cast her corpse aside as he turned his attention to Walt.

"This is all on you, Walt," Chad slurred as if what he had consumed of Sarah had made him drunk. "All I wanted was a little bit of fun. It wouldn't have killed Cally. She might even have enjoyed it if she would have given it a chance. But no, you couldn't let that happen, could you?"

"Damn right," Walt said defiantly, leveling the barrel of his shotgun at Chad and pumping a white phosphorous round into its chamber.

The thing that was Chad shook its head. "And what has being such a prude cost you, Walt? Sarah, Brent, Simon, and Lee … They're all dead now because of you. How does that feel?"

"I didn't kill them, Chad," Walt growled. "You did."

The glow of Chad's eyes became more intense as he snarled, "And I'll kill you too!"

Chad's hands reshaped themselves into masses of tentacles that shot outward, reaching for Walt. Walt blasted at them with his shotgun. The Dragon's Breath of the WP lit the tentacles ablaze.

Chad shrieked a high-pitched squeal that nearly blew out Walt and Cally's eardrums. His tentacles flailed about as Chad tried vainly to extinguish the burning fire that covered them.

Cally emptied the remainder of her pistol's magazine into Chad as careened about. Each shot tore into him, splattering globs of his ooze like blood across the hangar. His eyes came around onto her, glowing with pain-crazed anger.

"You little twit!" Chad howled. "How could you? Don't you know that I am going to be the best thing that's ever happened to you?"

Popping her pistol's empty magazine, Cally let it drop as she rammed another one into the weapon. "Walt! Now!" she shouted.

"One shot," Walt said as he took a step towards Chad. Their eyes met as Chad's connection with the game must have tipped him off to what was about to happen.

"No!" Chad wailed as Walt aimed at Chad's monstrous, horror-stricken face and ended him.

With the cheat code Cally had put in place for him powering his shotgun, he fired. The blast hit Chad dead on in his face. His entire head exploded in a shower of pus and gore. Walt walked over to stand over his corpse, the barrel of his shotgun leaking coils of smoke.

"Is he dead?" Cally asked.

"I think so." Walt looked over at her. His expression was a tired one and full of sadness.

"I ... I'm so sorry about Sarah," Cally told him.

"Me too," Walt said, wiping at his eyes.

"Walt," Cally said. "We need to be sure. Will you please burn what's left of him?"

"Sure thing," Walt replied. There were three more white phosphorus shells in his shotgun and he emptied them all into Chad. Each shot made Chad's headless body jerk as the hammered into it, setting it completely on fire. Walt backed away from the heat of the raging fire that Chad's body was being consumed by.

Walt and Cally watched it burn in silence. Cally reached to take his hand and clung to it tightly.

"It's over," she said quietly.

"Yeah," Walt agreed. "It really is."

Walt pulled free from Cally's grip on his hand and walked over to where Sarah's body rested on the hangar floor. Cally gave him his space as he said his goodbye. Walt wept openly as he finally let himself feel all the guilt, loss, and hurt that he had held in so long. His tears dripped onto Sarah's cheeks and he leaned over her. When he couldn't cry anymore, he knelt even closer to her still and kissed her a final time on the lips.

"I'm so sorry," he whispered, hoping she could hear him wherever her soul had departed to.

"She loved you, Walt," Cally said quietly, moving to place a hand on his shoulder.

"Let's go home," Walt said, getting to his feet.

Walt and Cally walked across the hangar to where the Beast sat and climbed inside it. Cally slid into the driver's seat as Walt took the one next to her. Solemnly, Cally cranked up the APC one final time and it vanished in a flash of light which transported it and them into the Hub.

The two of them exchanged brief goodbyes and a lingering hug before they downloaded themselves out of the game and were finally free of it at last.

****

Walt's connection to the game ended as he woke up in the real world for what felt like the first time in an eternity. His stomach greeted him a rumble of hunger. He didn't have a clue how long he been inside the game, but he knew it had been for far too long. His hands reached up to remove the neural interface helmet he wore. The living room of his apartment was dark and pale beams of moonlight crept in through the open window near his bookshelf. Walt sighed, taking a moment to remind himself that it really was all over with now. A cold breeze brushed against his skin as he got up from the couch and went to close the window. It was winter outside and the street below was covered in the white of freshly fallen snow.

Tomorrow, he would find Cally's number and give her a call to make sure she was okay but for right now, all he wanted to do was sleep. The nightmare was over. Walt closed the window and headed for his bedroom, vowing that his days of gaming were over with and that he would never upload himself into the system again.

END

Eric S Brown is the author of numerous book series including the Bigfoot War series, the Kaiju Apocalypse series (with Jason Cordova), the Crypto-Squad series (with Jason Brannon), the Homeworld series (With Tony Faville and Jason Cordova), the Jack Bunny Bam series, and the A Pack of Wolves series. Some of his stand alone books include Mecha, Kaiju Wars, Dropship Marines, War of the Worlds plus Blood Guts and Zombies, World War of the Dead, Last Stand in a Dead Land, Sasquatch Lake, Kaiju Armageddon, Megalodon, Megalodon Apocalypse, Kraken, Alien Battalion, The Last Fleet, and From the Ice They Came to name only a few. His short fiction has been published hundreds of times in the small press in beyond including markets like the Onward Drake and Black Tide Rising anthologies from Baen Books, the Grantville Gazette, the SNAFU Military horror anthology series, and Walmart World magazine. He has done the novelizations for such films as Boggy Creek: The Legend is True (Studio 3 Entertainment) and The Bloody Rage of Bigfoot (Great Lake films). The first book of his Bigfoot War series was adapted into a feature film by Origin Releasing in 2014. Werewolf Massacre at Hell's Gate was the second of his books to be adapted into film in 2015 and a film based on his book Cult of the Shadow People was released in 2017. Major Japanese publisher, Takeshobo, recently bought the reprint rights to his Kaiju Apocalypse series (with Jason Cordova) and it is slated for 2018 release in Japan. Ring of Fire Press will be releasing a collected edition of his Monster Society stories (set in the New York Times Best-selling world of Eric Flint's 1632) later this year. In addition to his fiction, Eric also writes an award winning comic book news column entitled "Comics in a Flash." Eric lives in North Carolina with his wife and two children where he continues to write tales of the hungry dead, blazing guns, and the things that lurk in the woods.

www.ingramcontent.com/pod-product-compliance
Lightning Source LLC
Chambersburg PA
CBHW052002170626
46808CB00007B/2737